Madame Storey's Way

by

Hulbert Footner

From: *Argosy All-Story Weekly*,
Vol. CXLI, No. 2 (March 11, 1922), p. 220.

Madame Storey's Way

Hulbert Footner

ESPRIOS DIGITAL PUBLISHING

CHAPTER 1.

I can not better put that extraordinary woman, my employer, before you than by describing my first meeting with her. It is easier to show her qualities in action than to describe them.

On a certain morning, no different from thousands of other mornings, I was in a train on my way to the office when eye was caught by this striking advertisement:

WANTED—By a woman of affairs, a woman secretary; common sense is the prime requisite.

Printed words have an extraordinary effect on one sometimes. Something in these terse phrases so strongly appealed to me that though I had a very good position at the time, I interrupted my journey to the office and went directly to the address given.

It was on Gramercy Square. The house proved to be one of the fine old dwellings down there that have been altered into chic more-orless-studio apartments. Bridal couples of the old Knickerbocker set are fond of setting up in that neighborhood, I am told. As I approached other females were converging at the door from three directions. The hall-boy, a typical New York specimen, looked us over with a grin, and without asking our business said:

"Madame Storey ain't down yet. Youse is all to wait in the little front room. "

I asked him privately what was Madame Storey's business.

"Search me! " he said cheekily. "She don't hang out no sign. "

Her apartment was the first floor front; part of the parlor floor of the old mansion. It was evidently only an office, but such an office! The walls were hung with priceless tapestries, there was an Italian Renaissance table for the secretary, ditto chairs for the clients, and here and there a bit of Chinese porcelain to make a vivid spot of color. I confess I looked a little dubiously at all this magnificence; somehow it didn't seem quite respectable. All the time I was wondering what Madame Storey's affairs consisted of.

There were about twenty women waiting; not nearly enough chairs, so most of us stood. It was funny to see how every Jill of them was busily cultivating an air of common sense. All looked at me as I entered with an expression which said as plainly as words:

"You might as well go; you will never do! " It was somewhat disconcerting until I saw that later arrivals received exactly the same look. No doubt I glared at them that way myself. There were far too many of us there already. What did more have to come for, we thought?

We were a motley throng ranging in age from seventeen to seventy. Women who obviously couldn't do a thing in this living world had rushed there to give Madame Storey the benefit of their common sense. One saw that there were as many definitions of common sense as there were women. Some thought it was sensible to paint their faces like a barber-pole; others, and these the larger number, considered that a sensible woman must cut her hair short, don a hideous travesty of masculine attire, and wrinkle up her forehead like an ape. As for myself, the moment I saw that exquisite interior, I realized the incongruity of my freckled, red-haired self amidst such surroundings. I had no hope of getting the position, but the whole affair was so funny to watch that I stayed on.

We waited an hour casting haughty glances at one another. But no one got tired and left. At the end of that time the boy from below threw open the door with a flourish and announced impressively:

"Madame Storey, ladies. "

There was a dramatic pause while we breathlessly waited with eyes fixed on the open door. Before we saw her we heard her voice—she was speaking to the boy outside, a slow voice with the arresting quality of the deeper notes of the oboe. Then she entered, and an audible breath escaped from all us women. I don't know what we expected, certainly not what we saw.

She was very tall and supremely graceful. It was impossible to think of legs in connection with her movements. She floated into the room like a shape wafted on the breeze. She was darkly beautiful in the insolent style that causes plainer women to prim up their lips.

She wore an extraordinary gown, a taupe silk brocaded with a shadowy gold figure, made in long panels that exaggerated her height and slimness, unrelieved by any trimming whatsoever. On her head she wore an odd little hat of the same color, with an exquisite plume curled around the' brim. All this was very well, but what made the women gasp was that snuggled in the hollow of her arm she carried a black monkey dressed in a coat of Paddy green, ' and a fool's cap hung with tiny gold bells.

She looked us over with eyebrows registering delicate mockery, and glanced at the ape as if to call his attention to the spectacle. Nevertheless she was not displeased by the sensation her entrance had created. I suspected that she had lingered outside especially to create that dramatic pause.

It was funny to see the faces of the waiting women, wherein strong disapproval struggled with the desire to please. As for myself having no pretensions to beauty, I don't have to be jealous of other women. I only knew the moment I laid eyes on Madame Storey that I wanted that job and wanted it badly. In the first place a really beautiful woman is an unfailing delight to my eyes; in the second something told me that whoever worked for that woman would see Life with a capital L. I didn't care much then what her business might be.

She had kept us waiting a long time, but once there she expedited matters. Without any preamble she turned to the woman nearest the door—it was one of the near-masculine type that I have mentioned, and said with a smile:

"There is no need of your waiting any longer. "

The woman gasped and turned a bricky color. "Why—why—" she began.

"I merely wished to save you from wasting more of your time, " said Madame Storey kindly.

The woman snorted, glared around at us all, grasped her umbrella firmly around the middle and stumped out.

The next one was a sweet young thing of forty-odd who put her head on one side and wriggled her shoulders when Madame Storey looked at her.

"You needn't wait, " said that lady.

The third was a middle-aged woman of determined mien. When Madame Storey turned to her she stiffened up—breathed hard and prepared to stand her ground.

Madame Storey shook her head with a deprecating smile.

"But I am a sensible woman, " insisted the other. "Everybody says there is no nonsense about me. "

Some of us were impolite enough to laugh.

"I don't doubt it, " said Madame Storey, but you are not what I require. "

"I insist on an explanation! "

"Certainly. You do not like me, you see. What would be the use? " The woman went out with a dazed air.

So it went. In five minutes the room was pretty well cleared. As she approached me my heart sank lower and lower, for I did want that job. But she appeared to overlook me altogether, and I was one of the three left when she completed her circuit. The other two were handsome, assured, well-dressed girls, and I told myself I had as good a chance against them as the traditional snowball down below.

Madame Storey said:

"I will see you young ladies one at a time in my own office. "

The other two pressed forward, each trying to be the first, but I hung back. I argued that she would not engage anybody until she had talked to all three, and as every lawyer knows there is considerable advantage in having the last say.

The first girl, a ladylike blonde in a tailored suit, was not inside more than two minutes. She came out looking red and flustered.

"Well? " we asked her simultaneously.

"Never gave me a chance to say a word! " she said crossly. "Offered me a cigarette. Since she offered it, I knew she must be a smoker, so I took it not to seem goody-goody. Well. I'm not accustomed to them. I choked over it. She just stood up and said good morning. "

The second girl looked wise, and went on in. But her interview didn't last more than thirty seconds. Reappearing, she burst out without even waiting for me to question her:

"The woman is crazy if you ask me! Offered me a cigarette, too. Well, I wasn't going to make the same mistake as the other girl. I declined. Said I didn't indulge. She just pointed to the inside of my right forefinger and stood up. It's just a little stained. What does she expect! Smokes like a furnace herself! "

I went into the next room with my heart jumping against the root of my tongue. It was a wonderful room: more like a little gallery in a museum than a woman's office; an up-to-date museum where they realize the value of not showing too much at once. With all its richness there was a fine severity of arrangement, and every object was perfect of its kind. I didn't appreciate all this at the moment. It was only as I came to know it that I realized the taste with which every object had been selected and arranged.

Madame Storey was seated at a great table with her back to the two windows. On the edge of the table was perched the little greenjacketed monkey, hands on knees and swinging his feet in an absurdly human way. He was gazing solemnly into his mistress's face and she was talking to him.

"Our last chance, Giannino. If this one fails us we'll have to go through with the whole silly business again to-morrow. "

The ape squeaked sympathetically, and gave me the once over.

She waved me to a chair. "What is your name? " she asked.

"Miss Brickley. "

"Your first name? It helps one to understand a person. "

"Bella. "

"Ah! " Giving me a shrewd look, she pushed a great silver box of cigarettes toward me.

I had already made up my mind what to do.

"Thanks, I don't smoke, " I said.

"Hope you don't object, " she said, taking one.

"No, indeed, " I answered. "I could acquire the habit as quickly as any one, but it would be an added expense. I have to think of that. "

"Ah! " she said, and let the matter drop. Anyhow, the cigarette had not tripped me.

She was regarding me searchingly. It was a kindly look, yet it made me frightfully uncomfortable. I hate people to stare at me, I am so plain. In spite of myself I burst out:

"I suppose you're thinking I wouldn't be much of an ornament to this establishment! "

"Yes, " she said quite coolly. "But I was also thinking, that you were not as bad as you thought yourself. Your hair is charming. "

My snaky red locks charming! I looked at the woman in astonishment.

"It would make an effective spot of color against my green tapestries, " she went on. "You know you don't have to drag it back from the roots like that. "

Her unexpectedness unnerved me a little. Unfortunately when I am nervous I get cross.

"Are you a sensible woman? " she asked with a bland air.

"I don't know, " I snapped. "I never gave the matter any thought. "

"That's encouraging. Tell me of what you were thinking when you came in just now. "

"Well, " I replied, "it was clear to me from the experiences of the two who preceded me that they had got themselves turned down by making pretenses; the first pretending that she smoked when she didn't, and the second pretending she didn't when she did. So I made up my mind not to bother about what you thought, but to be as nearly honest as I could. "

She laughed. "You hear that, my Giannino? "

The ape made a face at me. He and I never took to each other.

"Then you want this job? " Madame Storey asked.

"I do. "

"Why? "

"Because I think it's going to be exciting. "

She shrugged.

"I'll give you a trial, " she said casually.

I could scarcely believe my ears. Once I got there I had no doubt but that I could make myself indispensable.

"You have not only the rudiments of Sense, but a pretty spirit, " she added with that terribly searching gaze.

I was dumb.

"You are surprised that I praise you to your face? It is not my habit. But you, one can see, are suffering from mal-appreciation. Those two ugly lines between you brows were born of the belief that you were too plain and uninteresting ever to hope win a niche of your own in the world. And so you are if you think you are. But you don't have to think so. Think that cross look away and your face will show what is rarer than beauty, character, individuality. Old Time himself cannot rob you of that. " She turned to the ape. "I believe this is what we were looking for, Giannino. "

I felt as if this strange woman ha probed my soul.

"Are you employed now? " she asked abruptly.

"Yes. "

"What is your salary? "

I named it.

"I will double it, Miss Brickley. That is only fair, because I shall make great demands on you. "

I tried to stammer my thanks.

"Haven't you got some questions to ask me? " she said.

"What is the nature of your business? " I diffidently inquired.

"You will soon see, " she said smiling.

"I assure you it is quite honest. You may call me a practical psychologist—specializing in the feminine. "

CHAPTER 2.

Most of you will remember how the murder of Ashcomb Poor set the whole town agog. The victim's wealth and social position and the scandalous details of his private life that began to ooze out whetted the public appetite for sensation to the highest degree. For years Ashcomb Poor had been one of the most biogragraphed men in town, and now the manner of his taking off seemed like a tremendous climax to a thrilling tale.

The day it first came out in the papers Mme. Storey did not arrive at the office until noon. She was very plainly dressed and wore a thick veil that partly obscured her features. By this time I was accustomed to these metamorphoses of costume. From a little bag that she carried she took several articles and handed them over to me. These were (a) a hank of thin green string in a snarl, (b) a piece of iridescent chiffon, partly burned, (c) an envelope containing seven cigarette butts.

"Some scraps of evidence in the Ashcomb Poor case, " she explained. "Put them in a safe place. "

I had just been reading the newspaper report.

"What! Have we been engaged in that case already? " I exclaimed. Mme. Storey encouraged me to speak of our business in the first person plural, and of course it flattered me to do so.

"No, " she said, smiling, "but we may be. At any rate, I have forearmed myself by taking a look over the ground. "

In front of her room there was a smaller one that she used as a retiring and dressing room. She changed there now to a more suitable costume.

Two days later she remarked:

"The signs tell me that we shall receive a call from the district attorney's office to-day. "

Sure enough, Assistant District Attorney Barron turned up before the morning was over. Barron later became district attorney, it will be remembered. Though he was a young man for so big a job, he was a capable one, and held over through several succeeding administrations. This was the first time I had seen him, though it turned out he was an old friend of Mme. Storey's. A handsome, full-blooded fellow, his weakness was that he thought just a little too well of himself.

I showed him into the private office and returned to my desk. There is a dictograph installed between Mme, Storey's desk and mine, and when it is turned on I am supposed to listen in and make a transcript of whatever conversation may be taking place. Sometimes, to my chagrin, she turns it off at the most exciting moment, but more often she leaves it on, I am sure, out of pure good nature, because she knows I am so keenly interested. Mme. Storey is good enough to say that she likes me to be in possession of full information, so that she can talk things over with me.

The circuit was open now, and I heard him say:

"My God, Rose, you're more beautiful than ever! "

"Thanks, Walter, " she dryly retorted. "The dictograph is on, and my secretary can hear everything you say. "

"For Heaven's sake, turn it off! "

"I can't now, or she'd imagine the worst. You'll have to stick to business. I suppose you've come to see me about the Ashcomb Poor case. "

"What makes you jump to that conclusion? "

"Oh, you were about due. "

"Humph! I suppose that's intended to be humorous. If you weren't quite so sure of yourself you'd be a great woman, Rose. But it's a weakness in you. You think you know everything"

"Well, what did you come to see me about? "

"As a matter of fact, it was the Ashcomb Poor case. But that was just a lucky shot on your part. I suppose you read that I had been assigned to the case. "

"Walter, you're a good prosecutor, but you lack a sense of humor. "

"Well, you're all right in your own line, feminine psychology and all that. I gladly hand it to you. But the trouble with you is you want to tell me how to run my job too. "

"No one could do that, Walter. "

"What do you mean? "

"Never mind. How does the Poor case stand? "

"I suppose you've read the papers. "

"Yes; they're no nearer the truth than usual. Give me an outline of the situation as you see it. "

"Well, you know the Ashcomb Poors. Top-notchers; fine old family, money, and all that; leaders in the ultrasmart Prince's Valley set on Long Island. They have a small house out at Grimstead, where they made believe to live in quiet style; it's the thing nowadays. "

"In other words, the extravagantly simple life. "

"Exactly. They have no children. The household consisted of Mr. and Mrs. Poor, Miss Philippa Dean, Mrs. Poor's secretary, Mrs. Batten, the housekeeper, a butler and three maids; there were outside servants, too—chauffeur, gardener, and so on but they don't come into the case. Ashcomb Poor was a handsome man and a free liver. Things about him have been coming out—well, you know. On the other hand, his wife was above scandal, a great beauty. "

"Vintage of 1904. "

"Well, perhaps; but still in the running. These women know how to keep their looks. Very charitable woman and all that. Greatly looked up to. On Monday night Mrs. Poor took part in a big affair at the

Pudding-Stone Country Club near their home. A pageant of all nations or something. Her husband, who did not care for such functions, stayed at home. So did Miss Dean and Mrs. Batten. Mrs. Poor took the other servants to see the show. "

"There were only three left in the house, then? "

"Yes—Mr. Poor, Miss Dean, and Mrs. Batten. "

"Go on. "

"Mrs. Poor returned from the entertainment about midnight. Mrs. Batten let her in the front door. Standing there, the two women could see into the library, where Poor sat with his back to them. They were struck by something strange in his attitude, and started to investigate, Mrs. Batten in advance. "

"She was the first to realize that something had happened, and tried to keep Mrs. Poor from approaching the body. They struggled. Mrs. Poor screamed. The girl, Philippa Dean, suddenly appeared, nobody can tell from where. A moment later the other servants, who had gone around to the back door, ran in.

"Well, there was the situation. He had been shot in the back. The pistol was there. The butler telephoned to friends of the family and to the police. Grimstead, as you know, is within the city limits, so it comes within our jurisdiction. I was notified of the affair within an hour and ordered to take personal charge of the case. Nothing had been disturbed. I ordered the arrest of the Dean 'girl, and she is still in custody. "

"What do you want of me? " Mme. Storey inquired.

"I want you to see the girl. Frankly, she baffles me. Under our questioning she broke down before morning and confessed to killing the man. But the next day she repudiated her confession, and has obstinately stuck to her repudiation in spite of all we could do. I want you to see her and get a regular confession. "

"What about the girl's lawyer? "

"She has none as yet. Refused to see one. "

"You're sure she did it? "

"Absolutely. It was immediately apparent that the murder had been committed by one of the inmates of the house. "

"Why? "

"Because when Mr. Poor and the servants departed for the entertainment, Mrs. Batten, who let them out, turned on the burglaralarm, and it remained turned on until she let her mistress in again. One of the first things I did on arriving at the house was to make sure that the alarm was working properly. I also examined all the doors and windows. Everything was intact. "

"Why couldn't the housekeeper have done it? "

"A simple, timid old soul! Impossible! No motive. Besides, if she had she would hardly have given me the principal piece of evidence against those in the house; I mean her testimony about the burglar-alarm. "

"What motive could the girl have had? "

"The servants state that their master had been pestering her—forcing his attentions on her. "

"Ah! But this is all presumptive evidence, of course. What else have you? "

"Ashcomb Poor was shot with an automatic pistol belonging to Miss Dean. The butler identified it. At first she denied that it was hers. She could not deny, though, that she had one like it, and when asked to produce it she could not. It was not among her effects. "

"Where did you find the gun exactly? "

"In the dead man's hand. "

"In his hand? "

"Under his hand, I should say. It had been shoved under in a clumsy attempt to make it appear like a suicide. But the hand was clenched on top of the weapon. Moreover, the man was shot between the shoulders. He could not possibly have done it himself. The bullet passed completely through his body, and I found it lodged in the wall across the room. "

"Did the housekeeper hear the shot? "

"She did not. She was in another wing of the house. "

"Anything else against the girl? "

"Yes. When she appeared, attracted by Mrs. Poor's cry, though she was supposed to have retired some time before, she was fully dressed. Moreover, she knew what had happened before any one told her. "

"Ah! How does she explain these suspicious circumstances? "

"She will explain nothing. Refuses to talk. "

"What story did she tell when she confessed? "

"None. Merely cried out:

"'I did it! I did it! Don't ask me any more! '"

There was a silence here, during which Mme. Storey presumably ruminated on what she had been told. Finally she said:

"I'll see the girl, but it must be upon my own conditions. "

"What are those? "

"As an independent investigator, I hold no brief for the district attorney's office. "

"Well, there's no harm in that. "

"But you must understand what that implies. Neither you nor any of your men may be present while I am talking to her. And I do not bind myself to tell you everything she tells me. "

"That's out of the question. What would the old man say if he knew that I turned her over to an outsider? "

"Well, that's up to you, of course. " Mme. Storey spoke indifferently. "You came to me, you know. "

"Well—all right. " This very sullenly. "I suppose if she confesses you'll let me know. "

"Certainly. But I'm not at all sure this is going to turn out the way you expect. "

"After all I've told you? "

"Your case against her is a little too good, Walter. "

"Who else could have done it? "

"I don't know—yet. If she did it, why should she have stuck around the house until you arrested her? "

"She supposed it would be considered a suicide. "

"But, according to you, a year-old child wouldn't have been deceived into thinking so. "

"Well, you never can tell. They always do something foolish. Will you come down to the Tombs? I'll arrange for a room there. "

"No, I must see the girl here. "

"That's impossible! "

"Sorry; it's my invariable rule, you know. "

"But have a heart, Rose. I daren't let her out of my custody. "

"You and your men can wait outside the door, then. "

"It's most irregular. "

"I am an irregular person, " was the bland reply. "You should not have come to me. "

"Well—I suppose you must have your own way. "

"Always do, my dear. With the girl send a transcript of whatever statements have been taken down in the case. "

"All right. Rose, turn off that confounded dictograph, will you? I want to speak to you privately. "

"It's off. "

It wasn't though, for I continued to hear every word.

"Good God, Rose, why do you persist in trying to madden me? "

"Mercy, Walter! How? "

"You know! With your cold and scornful airs, your indifference. It's—it's only vanity. Your vanity is ridiculous! "

"Oh, if you're only going to call names, I'll turn on the dictograph! "

"No, don't, don't! I scarcely know what I'm saying, you provoke me so! Why won't you be decent to me, Rose? Why won't you take me? We were made for each other! "

"So you say. "

"Do you never feel anything, anything behind that scornful smile? Are you a breathing woman or a cold and heartless monster? "

"Bless me, I don't know. "

"You need a master! "

"Of course I do. Why don't you master me, Walter? "

"Don't taunt me. A man has his limits! You make me want to seize and hurt you. "

"Don't do that. You'd spoil my pretty frock. Besides, Giannino would bite the back of your neck. "

"Don't taunt me. You'd be helpless in my arms. You're always asking for a master. "

"I meant a master of my soul, Walter. "

"I don't understand you. "

"Yes, you do. Look at me! You can't. My soul is stronger than yours, Walter, and in your heart you know it. "

"You're talking nonsense! "

"Don't mumble your words. That's my tragedy, if you only knew it. I have yet to meet a man bold enough to face me down. How could I surrender myself to one whose soul was secretly afraid of mine? So here I sit. You know that the Madame I have hitched to my name is just to save my face. No one would believe that a woman as beautiful as I could be still unmarried—and respectable. But I am both, worse luck! "

"It's your own fault that you're alone. You think too well of yourself. You make believe to scorn all men. "

"Well, if it's a bluff, why doesn't some man call it? "

"I will right now! I'm tired of this fooling. You've got to marry me. "

"Look at me when you say that, Walter. "

A silence.

"Ah—you can't, you see. "

"Ah, Rose, don't torture me this way! Can't you see I'm mad about you? You spoil my rest at night; you come between me and my work by day. I hunger and thirst for you like a man in a desert. Think what a team you and I would make, Rose. There'd be no stopping us short of the White House. "

Here, to my chagrin, the dictograph was abruptly turned off, but when, a minute or two later, Mr. Barron burst out of the inner room purple with rage I guessed that no change had occurred in the situation. He flung across the floor and out of the door without a glance in my direction.

Mme. Storey called to me to bring in my notebook. As I entered she was talking to the monkey.

"Giannino, you are better off than you know. Better be a dumb beast than a half-thinking animal. "

The little thing wrinkled up his forehead and chirruped as he always did when she addressed him.

"You disagree with me? I tell you men would rather go to jail than put themselves to the trouble of thinking clearly. "

CHAPTER 3.

Eddie, the hall-boy, and I had become at least outwardly friendly. In his heart I think Eddie always despised me as "a Jane Gut of the storehouse, " one of his own expressions, but as he had the keenest curiosity about all that went on in our shop, he was obliged to be affable in order to tap such sources of information as I possessed. He adored Mme. Storey, of course; all youths did as well as older males. As for me, I couldn't help liking the amusing little wretch, he was so new.

Like most boys of his age his ruling passion was for airplanes and aviators. At this time his particular idol was the famous Lieutenant George Grantland who had broken so many records. Grantland had just started on a three days' point-to-point flight from Camp Tasker, encircling the whole country east of the Mississippi, and Eddie, in order to follow him, was obliged to buy an extra every hour. Bursting with the subject, and having no one else to talk to, he brought these up to my room. This was his style—of course I am only guessing at the figures.

"Here's the latest. Landed at New Orleans four thirty this A. M., two hours ahead of time. Gee! If I could only get out to a bulletin board! Slept four hours and went on. Four hundred and forty-two miles in under four hours. Wouldn't that expand your lungs? Say, that guy is a king of the air all right. Flies by night as well as day. They have lights to guide him where to land. Hasn't had to come down once for trouble. Here's a picture of his plane. It's the Bentley-Critchard type. They're just out. Good for a hundred and forty an hour. Six hundred horse. Do you get that? Think of driving six hundred plugs through the clouds. Some team! "

After two days of this I was almost as well acquainted with the exploits of Lieutenant Grantland as his admirer. Every hour or two Eddie would have a new picture of the dashing aviator to show me. Even after being snapshotted in the blazing sun and reproduced in a newspaper halftone, he remained a handsome young fellow.

Eddie was in the thick of this when they brought Philippa Dean up from the Tombs, but as she was indubitably a "class one jane, " his attention was momentarily won from his newspapers. The assistant district attorney did not accompany her. To be obliged to wait outside was, I suppose, too great a trial to his dignity. Miss Dean was under escort of two gigantic plain-clothes men, the slender little thing. I was glad, at any rate, that they had not handcuffed her. My first impression was a favorable one: her eyes struck you at once. They were large, full, limpid, blue, very wide open under fine brows, giving her an expression of proud candor in which there was something really affecting—however, I had learned ere this from Mme. Storey that you cannot read a woman's soul in her eyes, so I reserved judgment. Her hair was light brown. She was dressed with that fine simplicity which is the despair of newly arrived women. At present she looked hard and wary, and her lips were compressed into a scarlet line—but that was small wonder in her situation.

Mme. Storey came out when she heard them. What was her first impression of the girl I cannot say, for she never gave anything away in her face at such moments. She invited the two detectives to make themselves comfortable in the outer office, and we three women passed into the big room. She waved the girl to a seat.

"You may relax, " she said, smiling; "nobody is going to put you through the third degree here. "

But the girl sat down bolt upright, with her hands clenched in her lap. It was painful to see that tightness. Mme. Storey applied herself to the task of charming it away. She said to the ape:

"Giannino, take off your hat to Miss Dean, and tell her that we wish her well. "

The little animal stood up on the table, jerked off his cap and gibbered in his own tongue. It was a performance that never failed to win a smile, but this girl's lips looked as if they had forgotten how.

"The assistant district attorney has asked me to examine you, " Mme. Storey began in friendly style. "Being a public prosecutor he's bent on your conviction, having nobody else to accuse. But I may as well tell you that I don't share his feelings. Indeed, he's so cock-sure that it would give me pleasure to prove him wrong. "

I knew that my employer was sincere in saying this, but I suppose that the poor girl had learned to her cost that the devil himself can be sympathetic. At any rate, the speech had no effect on her.

"I hope you will believe that I have no object except to discover the truth, " Mme. Storey went on.

"That's what they all say, " muttered the girl.

"Satisfy yourself in your own way as to whether you can trust me. Come, we have all afternoon. "

"Am I obliged to answer your questions? " demanded the girl.

"By no means, " was the prompt reply, "Why don't you question me first? "

The girl took her at her word. "Who are you? " she asked. "I have been told nothing. "

"Mme. Rosika Storey. They call me a practical psychologist. The district attorney's office sometimes does me the honor to consult me, particularly in the cases of women. "

"You'll get no confession out of me! "

"I don't expect to. I don't believe you did it. No sane woman would shoot a man between the shoulder-blades and expect to make out that it was a suicide. At any rate, Ashcomb Poor seems to have richly deserved his fate. Come now, frankly, did you do it? "

The girl's blue eyes flashed.

"I did not. "

"Good! Then tell me what happened the night? "

The girl sullenly shook her head.

"What's the use? "

"Why, to clear yourself, naturally. "

"They haven't enough evidence to convict me. They couldn't convict me, because I didn't do it. "

"That's a perilous line to take, my dear. I suspect you haven't had much experience with juries. The gentlemen of the jury would consider silence in a woman not only unnatural, but incriminating. Of course they might let you off, anyway, if you condescended to ogle them, but as I say, it's perilous. Why did you confess in the first place? "

"To get rid of them. They were driving me out of my mind with their questions. "

"I can well understand that. Well then, what did happen, really? "

The girl set her lips. "I have made up my mind to say nothing, and I shall stick to it, " she replied.

Mme. Storey spread out her hands.

"Very well, let's talk about something else. Dean is a good old name here in New York. Are you of the New York family? "

"My people have lived here for four generations. "

"I have read of a great beau in the sixties and seventies Philip Dean. Are you related to him? "

"He was my grandfather. "

"I might have guessed it from your first name. How interesting! All the chronicles of those days are full of references to his wit and savoir faire. But he must have been a rich man. How does it come that you have to work for your living? "

"The usual story; the first two generations won the family fortune, and the next two lost it. I am of the fifth generation. "

"Well, I suppose one cannot have a famous *bon vivant* in the family for nothing. "

"Oh, no one could speak ill of my grandfather. He was a gallant gentleman. I knew him as a child. He spent his money in scientific experiments which only benefited others. My poor father was not to blame either. He lost the rest of the money trying to recoup his father's losses in Wall Street. "

"And you were thrown on your own resources. "

"Oh, I was never a pathetic figure. I could get work. There were always women, not very sure of themselves socially, who were glad to engage Philip Dean's grand-daughter. "

"That's how you came to go to Mrs. Poor? "

"No, that was different. Mrs. Poor didn't need anybody to tell her things. Her family was as good as my own. Her husband was traveling abroad and she was lonely. She engaged me as a sort of companion. "

"When did her husband return? "

The girl frowned.

"Now you think you're leading me up to it, don't you? " Mme. Storey laughed.

"I suspect you're the kind of young lady nobody can lead any further than she is willing to go. "

Miss Dean glanced suspiciously at me. "Is she taking down all I say? " she demanded.

"Not until I tell her to, " Mme. Storey replied.

"He returned two months ago. "

"Do you mind describing their house at Grimstead for me? " asked Mme. Storey, "There's no harm in that, is there? "

The girl shrugged. "No. It's a small house, considering their means, and it looks even smaller because of being built in the style of an English cottage, with low, overhanging eaves, and dormer windows. You enter through a vestibule under the stairs and issue into a square hall. This hall is two stories high and has a gallery running around three sides. On your left is the library; on your right the small reception room; the living-room, a large room, is at the back of the hall, with the dining-room adjoining it. These two rooms look out over the garden and the brook below. Between reception and dining room there is a passage leading away to the kitchen wing. Besides pantry, kitchen, and laundry, this wing has a housekeeper's room and a servants' dining-room. "

"And upstairs? "

"Mr. and Mrs. Poor's own suite is at the back of the house over the living room and dining room. My room is over the library. There is a guest room over the reception room. All the servant's rooms are in the kitchen wing. There is no third story. "

Mme. Storey affected to consult the notes on her desk. "Where was this burglar alarm that there has been so much talk about? "

"Hidden in a cranny between the telephone booth and the wall by the fireplace. The telephone booth was let into the wall just beyond the library door, and the fireplace is adjoining"

"Hidden, you say. Was there anything secret about it? "

"No. Everybody in the house knew of it. "

"What kind of switch was it? "

"It was just a little handle that lifted up and pulled down. When it was up it was off; when it was down it was on. "

"Describe the servants, will you? "

"How is one to describe servants? The butler, Briggs—well, he was just a butler; smooth, deferential, fairly efficient. The maids were just typical maids. None of them had been there long. Servants don't stick nowadays. "

"What about Mrs. Batten? "

In spite of herself the girl's face softened—yet at the same time a guarded tone crept into her voice. "Oh, she's different, " she said.

Mme. Storey did not miss the guarded tone. "How different? " she asked.

"I didn't look on Mrs. Batten as a servant, but as a friend. "

"Describe her for me? "

The girl, looking down, paused before replying. Her softened face was wholly charming. "A simple, kindly, motherly soul, " she said with a half-smile. "Rather absurd, because she takes everything so seriously. But while you laugh at her you get more fond of her. She doesn't mind being laughed at. "

"You have the knack of hitting off character! " said Mme. Storey. "I see her perfectly! "

I began to appreciate Mme. Storey's wizardry. Cautiously feeling her way with the girl she had discovered that Philippa had a talent for description in which she took pride—perhaps the girl aspired to be a writer. At any rate, when she was asked to describe anything, her eyes became bright and abstracted, and she forgot her situation for the moment.

It seemed to me that we were on the verge of stumbling on something, but to my surprise, Mme. Storey dropped Mrs. Batten. "Describe Mrs. Poor for me, " she asked.

"That is more difficult, " the girl said unhesitatingly. "She is a complex character. We got along very well together. She was always kind, always most considerate. Indeed, she was an admirable woman, not in the least spoiled by the way people kotowed to her. But I cannot say that I knew her very well, because she was always reserved—I don't mean with me, but with everybody. One felt sometimes that she would like to unbend, but had never learned how. "

"And the master of the house? "

The girl shuddered slightly. But still preoccupied in conveying her impressions, she did not take alarm. "He was a rich man, " she answered, "and the son of a rich man. That is to say, from babyhood he had never been denied anything. Yet he was an attractive man—when he got his own way; full of spirits and good nature. Everybody liked him—that is, nearly everybody. "

"Didn't you like him? " asked Mme. Storey.

"Yes, I did in a way—but—" She stopped.

"But what? "

She hung her head. "I'm talking too much, " she muttered.

Mme. Storey appeared to drop the whole matter with an air of relief. "Let's have tea, " she said to me. "I can see from Giannino's sorrowful eyes that he is famishing. "

I hastened into the next room for the things. Mme. Storey, in the way that she has, started to rattle on about cakes as if they were the most important things in the world.

"Every afternoon at this hour Miss Brickley and Giannino and I regale ourselves. We have cakes sent in from the pastry cooks. Don't you love cakes with thick icing all over them? I'm childish on the subject. When I was a little girl I swore to myself that when I grew up I would stuff myself with iced cakes. "

When I returned I saw that in spite of herself the girl had relaxed even further. Her eyes sparkled at the sight of the great silver plate of cakes. After all, she was a human girl, and I don't suppose she'd been able to indulge her sweet tooth in jail. Giannino set up an excited chattering. Upon being given his share he retired to his favorite perch on top of a big picture to make away with it.

While we ate and drank we talked of everything that women talk of: cakes, clothes, tenors and what-not. One would never have guessed that the thought of murder was present in each of our minds. The girl relaxed completely. It was charming to watch the play of her expressive eyes.

Mme. Storey, who, notwithstanding her boasted indulgence, was very abstemious, finished her cake and lighted the inevitable cigarette. Giannino stroked her cheek, begging piteously for more cake, but the plate had been put out of his way. Mme. Storey, happening to lay down her cigarette, Giannino, ever on the watch for such a contingency, snatched it up and clambered with chatterings of derision up to the top of his picture. There he sat with half-closed eyes blowing clouds of smoke in the most abandoned manner. Philippa Dean laughed outright; it was strange to hear that sound from her. I was obliged to climb on a chair to recover the cigarette. I spend half my time following up that little wretch. If I don't take the cigarette from him it makes him sick, yet he hasn't sense enough to leave them alone—just like many men I have known.

"Well, shall we go on with our talk? " asked Mme. Storey casually.

The girl spread out her hands. "You have me at a disadvantage, " she said. "It is so hard to resist you. "

"Don't try, " suggested my employer, smiling. "You may take your notes now, Miss Brickley. You needn't be afraid, " she added to the girl. "This is entirely between ourselves. No one else shall see them. You were saying that you liked Mr. Poor—with reservations. "

"I meant that one could have enjoyed his company very much if he had been content to be natural. But he was one of those men who pride themselves on their—their—what shall I say—"

"Their masculinity? "

"Exactly. And of course with a man of that kind a girl is obliged constantly to be on her guard. "

"The servants have stated that he pestered you with his attentions, " Mme. Storey remarked.

The girl lowered her eyes.

"They misunderstood, " she said. "Mr. Poor affected a very flowery, gallant style with all women alike; it didn't mean anything. "

Mme. Storey glanced at a paper on her desk. "The butler deposes that one evening he saw Mr. Poor seize you on the stairs and attempt to kiss you, and that you boxed his ears and fled to your room. "

Miss Dean blushed painfully and made no reply.

Mme. Storey, without insisting on one, went on: "What were the relations between Mr. and Mrs. Poor? "

"How can any outsider know that? " parried the girl.

"You can give me your opinion. You are a sharp observer. It will help me to understand the general situation. "

"Well, they never quarreled, if that's what you mean. They were always friendly and courteous toward each other. Not like people who are in love, of course, Mrs. Poor must have known what her husband's life was, but she was a religious woman, and any thought of separation or divorce was out of the question for her. My guess was that she had determined to take him as she found him, and make the best of it. Such a cold and self-contained woman naturally would not suffer as much as another. "

Have you knowledge of any incident in Mr. Poor's life that might throw light on his murder? "

"No. Nobody in that house knew anything of the details of this. He was not with us much. "

"Tell me about your movements on the night of the tragedy, " Mme. Storey urged.

But the girl's face instantly hardened. It is useless to ask me that, " she said. I do not mean to answer. "

But since you did not commit the crime why not help me to get you off? "

"I do not wish to speak of my private affairs which have nothing to do with this case. "

My heart beat faster. Here we were plainly on the road to important disclosures. But to my disappointment Mme. Storey abandoned the line.

"That is your right, of course, " she said. "But consider: you are bound to be asked these very questions in court before a gaping crowd. Why not accustom yourself to the questions in advance by letting me ask them. You are not under oath here, you know. You may answer what you please. "

This was certainly an unusual way of conducting an examination. Even the girl smiled wanly.

"You are clever, " she said with a shrug. "Ask me what you please. "

"What were you doing on the night of the tragedy? "

From this point forward the girl was constrained and wary again. She weighed every word of her replies before speaking. It was impossible to resist the suggestion that she was not always telling the truth.

"I was in my room. "

"The whole time? "

"Yes, from dinner until Mrs. Poor returned. "

"Why didn't you go to the pageant? "

"Those affairs bore me. "

"Had you not intended to go? "

"No. "

"Where was Mrs. Batten during the evening? "

"I don't know. In her room, I assume. "

"In what part of the house was that? "

"Her sitting room was downstairs in the kitchen wing. "

"An old woman. Wasn't she timid about being all alone in that part of the house? "

"I don't know. It did not occur to me. "

"You didn't see her at all during the evening? "

"No. "

"Where was Mr. Poor? "

"In the library, I understood. "

"All the time? "

"I'm sure I couldn't say. "

"Did you see him or have speech with him during the evening? "

"No. "

"There was nobody in the house but you three? "

"Nobody. "

"You're sure of that? "

"Quite sure. "

"The servants testified that when the alarm was raised you appeared fully, dressed. "

"That's nothing. It was only twelve o'clock. I was reading. "

"What were you reading? "

"Kipling's 'The Light that Failed. '"

"What became of the book? "

"I put it down when Mrs. Poor cried out. "

"Are you sure? It was not found in your room. "

"Of course I'm not sure. I may have carried it downstairs. I may have dropped it anywhere in my excitement. "

"Please describe the exact situation of your room. "

"It was in the northeast corner of the house. It was over the library. "

"Yet you heard no shot? "

"No. "

"That's strange. "

"The house is very well built; double floors and all that. "

"But immediately overhead? "

"I can't help that. I heard nothing. "

"You had no hint that anything was wrong until you heard Mrs. Poor's cry? "

"None whatever. "

"When she cried out what did you do? "

"I ran around the gallery and downstairs. "

"The gallery? "

"In order to reach the head of the stairs I had to encircle the gallery in the hall. "

"How long did it take you to reach Mrs. Poor's side? "

"How can I say? I ran. "

"How far? "

"Fifty or sixty feet; then the stairs. "

"Half a minute? "

"Perhaps. "

"What did you see when you got downstairs? "

"The stairs landed me at the library door. Just inside the door I saw Mrs. Batten clinging to Mrs. Poor. She was trying to keep Mrs. Poor from reaching her husband's side. "

"Mrs. Poor is a tall, finely formed woman, isn't she? "

"Yes. "

"Is Mrs. Batten a big woman? "

"No. "

"Strong? "

"No. "

"Yet you say she was able to keep her mistress back for half a minute? "

"You said half a minute. "

"Well, until you got downstairs. "

"So it seems. "

"Didn't that strike you as odd? "

"I didn't think about it. "

"Did you know what had happened? "

"Not right away. I soon did. "

"They told you? "

"No. "

"How did you guess, then? "

"From Mr. Poor's attitude, sprawling with his arms across the table, his head down—the pistol in his hand. "

"In his hand? "

"Well, under his hand, I believe. "

"Did you recognize it as your pistol? "

"I—I don't know. "

"Eh? "

"I mean I don't know just when I realized that it was mine. Pistols are so much alike. I hadn't handled mine much. "

"Well, how was it that it could be so positively identified as yours? "

"There were two little scratches on the barrel that somebody had put there before I got it. I had shown it to Mrs. Batten, and we had discussed what those two little marks might mean. Mrs. Batten must have spoken of it in the hearing of the servants. At any rate they knew about the marks. "

"How do you explain the fact that your pistol was in the dead man's hand? "

"I cannot explain it. "

"Where did you keep it? "

"In the bottom drawer of my bureau. "

"Was the drawer locked? "

"No. "

"When had you last seen it there? "

"Two days before when I—"

She stopped here.

"When you what? "

"When I put it away. "

"You'd had it out then? "

"Yes. "

"What for? "

"To have it fixed. "

"What was wrong with it? "

"I couldn't describe it, because I don't understand the mechanism. "

"Had you ever fired it? "

"No. "

"Then how did you know it was out of order? "

"I—I—" She hesitated.

"I won't answer that. "

"Surely that's a harmless question. "

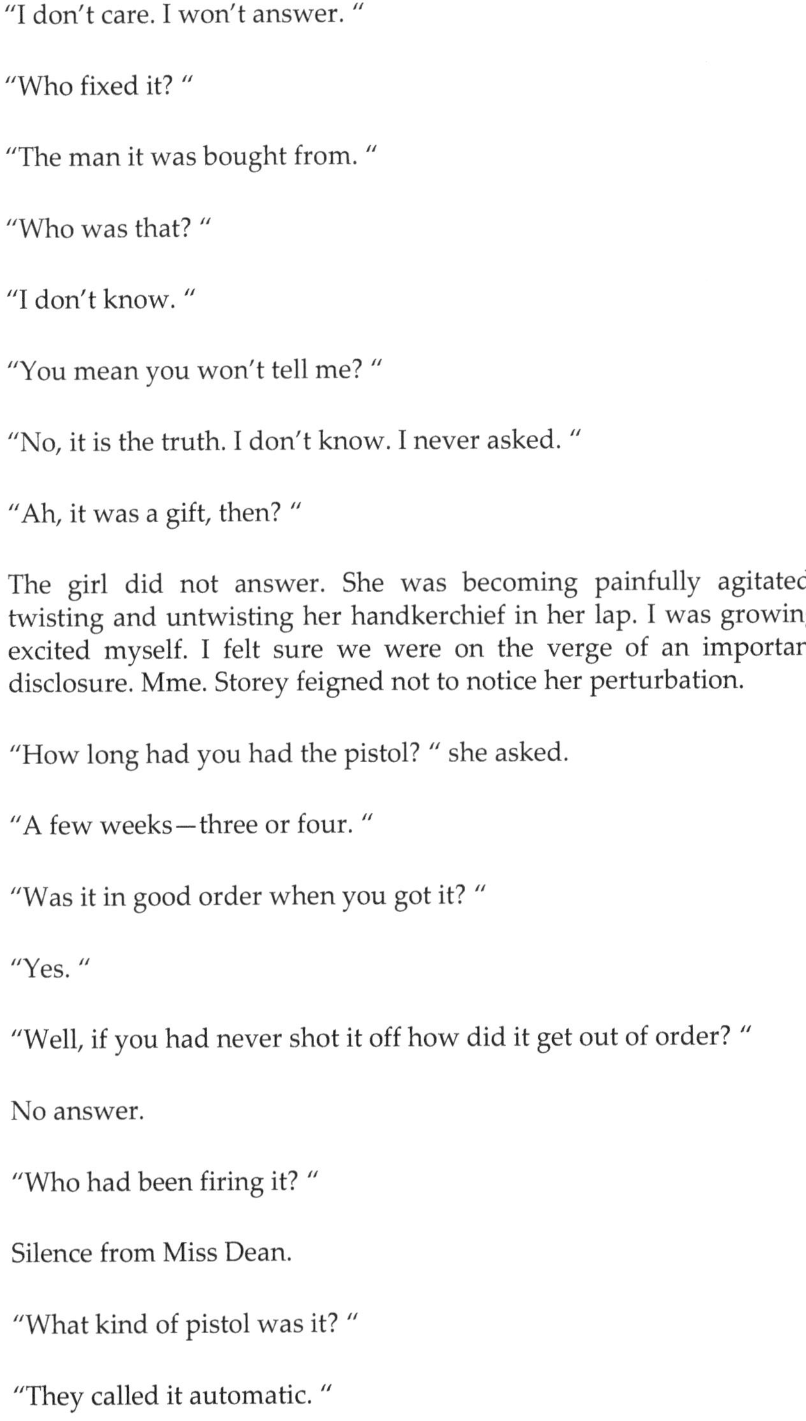

"I don't care. I won't answer. "

"Who fixed it? "

"The man it was bought from. "

"Who was that? "

"I don't know. "

"You mean you won't tell me? "

"No, it is the truth. I don't know. I never asked. "

"Ah, it was a gift, then? "

The girl did not answer. She was becoming painfully agitated, twisting and untwisting her handkerchief in her lap. I was growing excited myself. I felt sure we were on the verge of an important disclosure. Mme. Storey feigned not to notice her perturbation.

"How long had you had the pistol? " she asked.

"A few weeks—three or four. "

"Was it in good order when you got it? "

"Yes. "

"Well, if you had never shot it off how did it get out of order? "

No answer.

"Who had been firing it? "

Silence from Miss Dean.

"What kind of pistol was it? "

"They called it automatic. "

"What caliber? "

"I don't know. "

The next question came very softly.

"Who gave it to you, Miss Dean? "

I couldn't help but pity the poor girl, her situation was so extreme, and she was fighting so hard to control it.

"I won't answer that question. "

"It will surely be asked in court. "

"I won't answer it there. "

"Your refusal will incriminate you. "

"I don't care. "

"Tell them you found it, " Madame Storey suggested with an enigmatic, kindly look.

To my astonishment she arose, saying:

"That's all, Miss Dean. "

I couldn't understand it. The girl who was deathly pale and breathing with difficulty seemed on the point of breaking down and confessing the truth—yet she let her go. I confess I was annoyed with Mme. Storey. In my mind I accused her of neglecting her duty. The girl was no less astonished than I. Out of her white face she stared at my employer as if she could not credit her ears. Mme. Storey took a cigarette.

"Many thanks for answering my questions, " she said. "I see quite clearly that you couldn't have done this thing. I shall tell the assistant district attorney so. "

The girl showed no gratitude at this assurance, but continued to stare at Mme. Storey with hard anxiety and suspicion. I stared too. It was perfectly clear to me that Philippa Dean had guilty knowledge of the murder.

"We'll have to hand you back to your watchdogs now, " said Mme. Storey. "Keep up a good heart. "

The girl went out like one in a dream.

When the plain-clothes men took her Mme. Storey and I sat down again and looked at each other. She laughed.

"Bella, you look as if you were about to burst. Out with it! "

"I don't understand you! " I cried.

"Didn't you think she was a charming girl? "

"Yes, I did. I was terribly sorry for the poor young thing, but—"

"But what? " I took my courage in my hands and continued:

"You mustn't let your compassion for her influence you. You have your professional reputation to think of! "

"You are more jealous of my professional reputation than I am, " she said teasingly.

"Why did you stop just when you did? "

"Because I had found out what I wanted to know. "

"What had you found out that Mr. Barron had not already told you? She was just—at the point of—"

"Of repeating her confession? "

"I'm sure of it! "

"That is just what I wanted to forestall, Bella. Another confession would simply, have complicated matters. "

I simply stared at her.

"Because she didn't do it, you see, Bella. "

"Then why should she confess? "

My employer merely shrugged.

"How can you be so sure she didn't do it? Anybody could see she was lying. "

"Certainly she was lying. "

"Well, then? "

"It was by her lies that I knew she was innocent. "

"You are just teasing me, " I said.

"Not at all. Read over your notes of her answers. It's all there, plain as a pikestaff. "

I read over my notes, but saw no light.

"That unmistakably guilty air, " I said. "How do you explain that? "

"I wouldn't call it a guilty air. "

"Well, anxious, terrified. "

"That's more like it. "

"Even if she didn't do it she knows who did. "

"Possibly. "

"Then why didn't you make her tell you? "

"Sometimes young girls have to be saved from themselves, Bella. " And that was all I could get out of her.

CHAPTER 4.

The moment Philippa Dean got back to Headquarters Mr. Barron must have started for our office. He arrived within forty minutes. When I showed him into Mme. Storey's room I followed, for since the violent interview of the morning she had instructed me to be present whenever he was there.

He was furious at what he regarded as my intrusion. He said nothing, but glared at me and I breathed a silent prayer that I might not fall into the clutches of the district attorney's office, at least as long as he was there. He sat down crossing and uncrossing his legs, slapping his knee with his gloves, and scowling sidewise at Mme. Storey from under beetling brows. Giannino, who detested him, fled to the top of his picture, where he sat hurling down imprecations in the monkey language at the man's head, and looking vainly around for something more effective to throw.

Mme. Storey was in her most impish mood. "Lovely afternoon, Walter, " she remarked mellifluously.

He snorted.

"Will you have some tea? We've had ours. "

"No, thank you. "

"A cigarette, then? " She pushed the box toward him.

"You know I never use them. "

"Well, you needn't be so virtuous about it. " She took one herself.

The graceful movement with which she stuck it in her mouth never failed to fascinate me—him, too.

He was silent. Mme. Storey blew a cloud of smoke. He scowled at her in a sullen, hungry way. I was sorry for the man. Really, she used him dreadfully.

"Rose, how many of those do you use a day? " he abruptly demanded.

"Oh, not more than fifty, " she drawled, with a wicked twinkle in my direction.

She may have spoiled half that many a day, but she never took more than a puff or two of each.

"You're ruining your complexion, " he said.

"Mercy! " she cried in mock horror, snatching up the little gold-backed mirror that always lay on her table. She studied herself attentively. "It does show signs of wear. What can one expect? It's six hours old already. "

From her little bag she produced rougestick, powder-puff, pencils, et cetera, and nonchalantly set about using them. I might remark that Mme. Storey had developed the art of making-up to an extraordinary degree of perfection. In the beginning I had refused to believe that she used any artificial aids until the process took place before my eyes.

Absolutely indifferent to what people thought, she was likely to lug out the materials at any time, but particularly when she desired to be delicately insulting.

Mr. Barron became, if possible, angrier than before. His instinct told him, of course, that no woman would reveal her beauty secrets to a man unless she were indifferent to what he thought. For a moment or two he fumed in silence, then said:

"Please put those things away. I want to talk to you. "

"You told me my complexion needed repair, Walter. Go ahead. Making-up is purely a subconscious operation. I'm listening. "

They were a strong-willed pair. She would not stop making up, and he would not speak until she gave him her full attention. There was a long silence. It was rather difficult for me. I sat at my little table, making believe to busy myself with my papers. Mme. Storey put aside the cigarette. That little scamp Giannino came sneaking down, but I got it first, and clapped it in the ash-jar with a cover that he cannot open. He retired, sulking, into a corner, and swore at me in his way.

Mme. Storey finally put down the mirror. "Is that better, Walter? " she asked, with a wicked smile.

He puffed out his cheeks.

"I'm waiting to hear you, " she said, putting away the make-up.

"It's a confidential matter, " he rejoined, glancing at me.

"Miss Brickley knows all about the Poor case, " she said carelessly. "You needn't mind her. "

"Well, what happened? " he asked sullenly.

"Nothing much. "

"Did you get a confession from the girl? "

"No; I managed to forestall it. "

His jaw dropped. "What do you mean? "

"She was just on the point of making a confession when I sent her back to you. "

"Will you be so good as to explain yourself? "

"A confession would simply have puffed you up, Walter, and obstructed the ends of justice. Because she didn't kill Ashcomb Poor. "

"I suppose you had your secretary take notes of her examination, " he said. "Please let her read them to me. "

Mme. Storey shook her head.

"The girl talked to me in confidence, Walter. "

"But surely I have the right—"

"We agreed beforehand, you know. "

The assistant district attorney, very angry indeed, muttered something to the effect that he "would know better next time. "

"That, of course, is up to you, " she said sweetly. "Anyway, it wouldn't do any good to read you the notes, because I brought out no new facts of importance. "

"Then how do you know she's innocent? " he demanded.

"By intuition, " she said with her sweetest smile.

He flung up his hands.

"Good Heaven! Can I go into court with your intuition? "

"I suppose not. But so much the worse for the court. I haven't much of an opinion of courts, as you know, for the very reason that they throw out intuition. They choose to found justice solely on reason, when, as every sensible person knows, reason is the most fallible of human faculties. You can prove anything by reason. "

To this Mr. Barron hotly retorted:

"Yet I never saw a lying woman in court but who, when she was caught, did not fall back on her so-called intuition. "

"That may be. But because there are liars is not to say there is no truth. Intuition speaks with a still small voice that is not easy to hear."

"Does your intuition inform you who did kill Ashcomb Poor? " he asked sarcastically.

"I shall have to have more time for that, " she parried.

"I thought your intuition was an instantaneous process. "

"Since you force me to meet you on your own ground, I must have sufficient time to build up a reasonable case. "

"Aha! Then you don't despise reason altogether. "

"By no means. But my reasoning is better than yours because it is guided by the voice of intuition. "

"Do you expect me to release this girl on the strength of your intuition? "

"By no means. She'd run away. And we may need her later. "

"Run away! This paragon of innocence? Impossible! "

"There are a good many things that reasonable men do not understand, " drawled Mme. Storey. "Take it from me, though, in the end you will come off better in this affair if you simply hold the girl in the House of Detention as a material witness. "

"Thanks, " he said; "but I am going before the grand jury tomorrow to ask for an indictment for homicide. "

"As you will! Men must be reasonable. According to your theory, she killed him in defending herself from his attentions, didn't she? "

"That's what I intimated. "

"Well, as a reasonable man, how do you account for the fact that she was willing to stay in the house with him alone except for the old housekeeper? "

"The point is well taken, " he admitted, but with a disagreeable smile that suggested he meant to humble her later. Mme. Storey continued:

"Moreover, she must have put herself in the way of his attentions, for the tragedy occurred in the man's own library. "

"I confess that that stumped me at first, " he said, "likewise the fact that he had apparently been shot unawares. But since this morning some new evidence has come to light. "

He waited for her to betray curiosity, but she, who read him like a book, only blew smoke.

"Ashcomb Poor's will was read this morning. "

"Yes? "

"He left Philippa Dean ten thousand dollars. "

Mme. Storey betrayed not the slightest concern.

"As a testimony to her sterling characters, no doubt, " she murmured.

"Character nothing! " was the retort.

"Well, as far as that goes, Ashcomb Poor's motives do not concern me. The salient fact to me is that the girl knew she was down in his will. "

"When was the will dated? "

"Three days before his death. "

"Well, she didn't lose any time! How did she know she was named in it? "

"It appears that Ashcomb Poor in his cups talked about the different bequests to his butler, who witnessed the document. The butler told Mrs. Batten, and Mrs. Batten told the girl. "

"Was Mrs. Batten mentioned in the Will? "

"Yes, for five thousand. "

"Perhaps she killed Ashcomb Poor. "

"Ridiculous! "

Chapter 5.

Mme. Storey decided that we must interview all the material witnesses in this case.

My desk in the outer office was beside the window. Next morning while I was awaiting the arrival of my employer I saw an elegantly appointed town car draw up below, and a woman of exquisite grace and distinction got out. She was dressed and veiled in the deepest mourning, and I could not see her face, but, guessing who it was, I experienced a little thrill of anticipation. The door was presently thrown open by Eddie—it was only visitors of distinction that he condescended to announce. "Mrs. Poor to see Mme. Storey. "

I jumped up in a bit of fluster. What would you expect? The famous Mrs. Ashcomb Poor, of whom so much had been written; her beauty, her dresses, her jewels, her charities, and now her tragic bereavement! How I longed to see her face. She made no move to put aside her veil, though.

"Mme. Storey not in? " she said in a disappointed voice.

"I am expecting her directly, " I said. She will be very much disappointed to miss you. "

"I do not at all mind waiting, " Mrs. Poor replied.

Her voice was as crisp and clear as glass bells. I brought a chair forward for her. I knew I ought to have shown her directly into the adjoining room, but I did want to get a good look at her. Her simple black dress had been draped by a master artist. I cudgeled my brain to think of some expedient to tempt her to put back her veil. I offered he a magazine, but she waved it aside, thanking me. My ingenuity failed me. It was hardly my place to start a conversation.

Mme. Storey was not long in arriving. She was all in black too, I remember, but it was black with a difference; there was nothing of the mourner about her. And Giannino, who, poor wretch, had to dress to set off his mistress, was wearing a coat and cap of burnt orange.

My employer expressed her contrition at keeping Mrs. Poor waiting, and led that lady directly into the adjoining room. Alas! I was not bidden to follow. I would have given a good deal to be able to watch and listen to the conversation between those two extraordinary women.

I remained at my desk in the deepest disappointment. Suddenly I heard the dictograph click. With what joy I snatched up the headpiece and pulled notebook and pencil toward me!

At least I was to hear.

Mme. Storey was saying:

"It was awfully good of you to consent to come to a strange woman's office. I should not have asked it had I not thought that my coming to you would only have been an embarrassment. "

"I was very glad to come, " Mrs. Poor replied in her bell-like voice. "You are not by any means unknown to me. On every side one hears of the wonderful powers of Mme. Storey. I was very much pleased to hear that you had interested yourself in my unhappy affairs. One longs to know the truth and have done with it. One can rest then, perhaps. "

"And you are willing to answer my questions? "

"Most willing. "

"This is really good of you. For of course it's bound to be painful, though I will spare you as far as I am able. If I trespass too far you must rebuke me. "

"There is nothing you may not ask me, Mme. Storey. "

"Thanks. I'll be as brief as possible. No need for us to go over the whole story. I am already pretty well informed from the police and from my examination of Miss Dean yesterday. "

"Ah, you have seen the girl? " put in Mrs. Poor.

"Yes. "

"What did she say? "

"Nothing but what has been published. "

"Poor, poor creature! "

"You do not feel unkindly toward her? "

"My feelings toward her—are very mixed. I could not see her, of course. But I feel no bitterness. How do I know what reason she may have had? And to convict her will not restore my husband to life. "

"You have known Miss Dean a long time? "

"Since she was a child. Her family and mine have been acquainted for several generations. "

"Has Miss Dean a love affair? "

"No, nothing serious. "

"You are sure? "

"Quite sure. I must have known it if she had. Several of the young men who frequented our house paid her attention—a pretty girl, you know—but not seriously. "

"I should have thought—"

"I'm afraid young men are worldly minded nowadays, " said Mrs. Poor. "She had no money, you see. "

"Now I come to a painful subject, " said Mme. Storey compassionately. "I am sorry to have to ask you, but I am anxious to establish the exact nature of the relations between your husband and Miss Dean. "

"You need not consider me, " murmured Mrs. Poor. "I have to face the thing. "

"Some of the servants have given evidence tending to show that your husband was infatuated with her. "

"I'm afraid it's true. "

"What makes you think so? "

"One learns to read the man one lives with his looks, the tones of his voice, his little unconscious actions. "

"You have no positive evidence of his wrong-doing; you never surprised him, or intercepted notes? "

"That would not be my way, " said Mrs. Poor proudly.

"Of course not. I beg your pardon. "

Mrs. Poor went on bitterly:

"If I had wanted evidence against him plenty of it was forced on me—I mean in other cases. "

"Nothing that could be applied to this case? "

"No. "

"Then we needn't go into that. How did the girl receive his overtures? "

"As an honest girl should. She repulsed him. "

"How do you know? "

"I knew in the same way that I knew about him—from her actions day by day; her attitude toward him. "

"What was that? "

"On guard. "

"That might have been interpreted either way, might it not? "

"Oh, yes. But there was her attitude toward me—open, affectionate, unreserved. "

"That might have been good acting, " suggested Mme. Storey.

"It might, but I prefer not to think so. "

"You have a good heart, Mrs. Poor. How long had this been going on? "

"About a month. "

"But if the girl was sincere, how do you account for the fact that she was willing to put up with this intolerable situation? "

"Very simply; she needed the money. "

"But if she'd always been well employed why should she be so hard up? "

"She has responsibilities. She supports two old servants of her mother's, who are no longer able to work. "

"Ah! But how could you tolerate the situation, Mrs. Poor? "

"You mean why didn't I send her away? How could I turn her off? Ever since I realized what was going on I have been trying to find her a situation with one of my friends, but they thought if I was willing to let her go there must be something undesirable about her."

"Naturally. Was that the only reason you kept her? "

Mrs. Poor's answer was so low it scarcely carried over the wire.

"No; I wish to be perfectly frank with you—I confess, as long as she was there I knew in a way what was going on, but if she had gone away—You see—"

"Then you did have some doubt of her? "

"My husband was a man very attractive to women. He was accustomed to getting his way. I was thinking of her more than of myself. His fancies never lasted long. "

"Did you know that he had put her in his will? "

"Not until the will was read yesterday. "

"What do you suppose was his motive in doing that? "

"How can one say? "

"May it not have been merely for the purpose of annoying you? "

"Possibly. He was not above it. "

"Now, Mrs. Poor, with the situation as it was, how could you bring yourself to leave the girl alone with him except for the housekeeper?"

"That was not my fault. It was sprung on me. I had no time to plan anything. "

"What do you mean? "

"It had been understood up to the last moment that Mr. Poor was to accompany me to the entertainment. But at dinner he begged off. What could I do? I had to go myself because I was taking a prominent part. "

"Then why didn't you ask her to go with you? "

"I did. "

"And she wouldn't? "

"She wouldn't. "

"Why? "

"She said she had no dress in order. "

"Did you believe that? "

"No. "

"You suspected that this staying home might have been pre-arranged? "

"Oh, I wouldn't go as far as that. "

"But if it were not prearranged why should she have gone to the library? "

"Who can tell what happened? He might have sent for her on the pretext of dictating letters. He had done that before. "

"You seek to excuse her. That doesn't explain why she chose to stay at home after she knew he was going to be there. "

"Perhaps she was excited—thrilled by his infatuation; girls are like that. Perhaps she was curious to see how he would act—confident in her power to restrain him. And found out too late that she was up against elemental things, and was obliged to defend herself. "

"But she must have had some inkling of what was likely to happen, since she took her pistol with her when she went to the library. Did you know that she possessed a pistol? "

"No. "

"Now, Mrs. Poor, let us jump to your return home that night. Describe your homecoming as explicitly as possible. "

"It was five minutes past midnight. I am sure of the time because I glanced at the clock as I was leaving the club. It was five minutes before the hour then. It took us about ten minutes to cover the three miles, for the road was thronged with returning motors. "

"One minute; the entertainment was held in the open air, wasn't it? "

"Yes, and we dressed in the club-house. We had the limousine. I rode with my own maid, Katy Birkett, beside me, and the cook and the housemaid opposite. The butler was outside with the chauffeur. When we reached home I got out alone at the front door. I told the others to drive along to the service door, because I thought it might annoy Mr. Poor to have them trooping through the house. The car waited there until the door was opened, because they didn't want to leave me standing there alone in the dark. "

"Mrs. Batten opened the door. This surprised me, because she was usually in bed long before that hour. I had expected my husband to let me in. I had had the chauffeur sound his horn in the drive to give notice of our coming.

"I said to Mrs. Batten:

"'Why aren't you in bed? '

"She answered that she thought she'd better wait up—or something like that. I asked her where Mr. Poor was, and she said he had fallen asleep in the library.

"A few steps from the inner door I could see into the library. The door was standing open, as it had been when I left. I could see my husband sitting at his writing table in the center of the room, his back to the door. His head was lying on his arms, and I, too, thought he was asleep. I noticed the fire had gone out. "

"Oh, there had been a fire? "

"Yes, Mr. Poor liked to have a wood fire in the library except in the very hottest weather. As Mrs. Batten removed my cloak I called to him, 'Wake up, Ashcomb! You'll get stiff, sleeping like that. '"

"He did not move. Mrs. Batten and I were simultaneously struck by the suspicion that something was the matter. We both started toward him. I had not taken two steps before I saw—oh! —a ghastly dark stain on the rug beneath his chair. I saw the pistol. An icy hand seemed to grip my throat. I stopped, unable to move. The room turned black before me. "

"You fainted? "

"No. It was only for a second. I started forward again. Mrs. Batten turned and blocked my way. 'Don't go! Don't go! ' she cried. Then something seemed to break inside me. I screamed. Then Miss Dean was there. I didn't see her come. I clung to her—"

"One moment. After you screamed how long was it before Miss Dean came? "

"No time at all. She was right there. "

"You are sure? "

"Quite sure. "

"Perhaps you had cried out before without knowing it. "

"Impossible. With that icy grip on my throat. "

"Well, go on please. "

"I—I broke down completely then. It was so awful a shock, and—and that dark, wet stain on the rug! The other servants ran in from the back of the house. The maids set up an insensate screaming. Somebody got them out again. The butler examined my—the—the body. He said he was quite dead—cold. I had sufficient presence of mind to order that nothing in the room be touched. I had the man telephone my brother, who lives near, and our doctor—just to be sure. The servants helped me upstairs; people began to come—the police. My recollection is not very clear after that. "

"Were you present when the police examined the servants and Miss Dean? "

"No. "

"When did you first begin to suspect her? "

"In the morning when I asked for her they told me she had been arrested. That was a fresh shock. I had supposed it was suicide. Ionly learned the facts little by little, because people didn't want to talk to me about it and I hadn't the strength to insist. "

"Did you notice anything peculiar in Miss Dean's manner when she came to you? "

"Not at the time, of course. I was too distracted. But when I thought about it later, she was strangely agitated. "

"Well, you all were, of course. "

"She was different. Hers was not the impersonal horror and dismay of the servants; hers was a personal feeling. She seemed about to faint with terror; she could, hardly speak. She was not surprised. "

"What did she say to you? "

"She, too, tried to keep me back. She said, 'Don't go to him. It's all over. ' At the moment I thought nothing of it. Afterward it occurred to me that none of us had been near him then. We didn't know he was dead until the butler came. "

"That is very significant, " said Mme. Storey.

This ended Mrs. Poor's examination.

After the exchange of some further civilities she came out of the inner room. Her veil was pushed aside and I had my wished for chance to see her face. Her voice over the wire had been so cool and collected that I was not prepared for what I saw. A truly beautiful woman with proud, chiseled features, the events of the last few days had worked havoc there. There were dark circles under her eyes, and deep lines of suffering from her nose to her mouth. I realized how profoundly humiliating the disclosures, following upon the murder, must have been to her proud soul. Seeing my eyes on her face, she quickly let the veil fall and went out without speaking.

As a result of the examination of Mrs. Poor I will not deny that I felt a certain satisfaction. Greatly as I admired my employer I was not sorry to see her proved wrong for once. It is not the easiest thing in the world to get along with a person who is always right. Mme. Storey's insistence on Philippa Dean's innocence had provoked me just a little. Mme. Storey made no reference to what had taken place between her and Mrs. Poor, and of course I did not gloat over her.

CHAPTER 6.

An hour after Mrs. Poor had departed I heard a timid tap on my door, and upon opening it beheld a round little body in a stiff black dress and a funny little hat with ostrich tips. She carried her gloved hands folded primly on the most protuberant part of her person, and from one arm hung a black satin reticule. She had cheeks like withered rosy apples, and short-sighted eyes peering through thick glasses. There was a wistful, childlike quality in her glance that immediately appealed to one. At present the little lady was scared and breathless.

"Does Mme. Storey live here? " she gasped.

"This is her office, " I said. "Come in. "

"I am Mrs. Batten. "

I looked at her with strong interest.

"Mme. Storey will be glad to see you, " I said.

"I told her I'd come, " she faltered; "but I'm so upset—so upset, I'm sure if she asks me the simplest questions my wits will fly away completely. "

"You needn't be afraid of her, " I said soothingly.

I knew whereof I spoke. The instant Mme. Storey laid eyes on the trembling little body, she smiled and softened. She put away her worldly airs and was just like simple like folks. I remained in the room. Mme. Storey talked of indifferent matters until Mrs. Batten got her breath somewhat, and brought the matter very gradually around to the Poor case. At the first reference to Philippa Dean the tears started out of the old eyes and rolled down the withered cheeks.

"My poor, poor girl! " she mourned. "My poor girl! "

"You were very fond of her then? " put in Mme. Storey gently.

"Like a daughter she was to me, madame. "

"Well, let's put our heads together and see what we can do. You can help me a lot. First of all, where were you all evening while Mrs. Poor was at the entertainment? "

With a great effort Mrs. Batten collected her forces and called in her tears. Her hands gripped the arms of her chair.

"I was in my room, " she said; "my sitting room downstairs. "

"All alone? "

"Why, of course. "

"Please tell me just where your room is. "

"Well, the way to it from the front hall is through a door between the reception room and the dining room and along a passage. Halfway down this passage is my door on the right and the pantry door opposite. At the end of the passage another passage runs crosswise. That we call the back hall. It has a door on the drive—"

"That is the door by which the servants entered when they returned with Mrs. Poor? "

"Yes, madame. And at the other end of the back hall there's a door to the garden. The back stairs are in this hall. The kitchen and the servants' dining room are beyond. "

"I get the hang of it. Wasn't it unusual for you to remain up so late? "

"Yes, it was. "

"How did it happen? "

"Well—I got interested in a book. "

"What book? "

Mrs. Batten put a distracted hand to her brow.

"Let me see—my poor wits! Oh, yes, it was called 'The Light That Failed. '" No muscle of Mme. Storey's face changed. "

"Ah! An admirable story! I know it well! What I particularly admire is the opening chapter, where the young man steps out of the clock case and confronts the thief in the act of rifling the safe. "

"I thought that a little overdrawn, " said Mrs. Batten.

I gasped inwardly. I could scarcely believe my ears. Our dear, gentle little old lady was lying like a trooper, and Mme. Storey had trapped her. For, of course, as everybody knows, there is no such scene in "The Light That Failed. " Mme. Storey went right on:

"Please tell me exactly what happened when Mrs. Poor returned that night. "

Mrs. Batten complied. Up to a certain point her story tallied exactly with that of her mistress, and there is no need for repeating it. Mrs. Batten corroborated Mrs. Poor's statement that Philippa Dean had appeared as soon as Mrs. Poor cried out.

Then Mme. Storey said:

"But Miss Dean testified that she had to run all the way around the upstairs gallery and downstairs. "

Mrs. Batten gave her a frightened look. "Oh, well, I may be mistaken, " she said quickly. "It was all so dreadful. Maybe it was a minute before she got there. "

"What did Miss Dean say to Mrs. Poor when she got there? "

"She didn't say anything—that is, not anything regular. She put her, arm around her and said, 'Be calm! '—or 'Don't give way, ' or something like that. "

"Didn't Miss Dean say, 'Don't go to him. It's all over. '"

Mrs. Batten sat bolt upright in her chair, and the near-sighted eyes positively shot sparks.

"She did not say that! "

"Can you be sure? "

"I'll swear it! "

"She might have said it without your hearing. "

"I was there all the time. I had hold of Mrs. Poor, too. "

"But Mrs. Poor has testified that Miss Dean said that. "

The old woman obstinately primmed her lips.

"I don't care! "

"Wouldn't you believe your mistress? "

"Not if she said that. She was mistaken. She was half wild anyway. She didn't know what anybody said to her.

"Why, nobody knew that Mr. Poor was dead then. Not till the butler came. "

Mrs. Batten's anxiety on the girl's behalf was so obvious that her testimony in the girl's favor did not carry much weight.

Mme. Storey continued:

"Did you notice anything strange about Miss Dean's manner when she came? "

Mrs. Batten sparred for time.

"What do you mean? " she asked.

"Was she unduly agitated? "

"Why, of course, we all were. "

"I said unduly. Did she behave any differently from the others? "

The little old lady began to tremble.

"What are you trying to get me to say? " she stammered.

"She didn't do it! She couldn't have done it! That sweet young girl, so gentle, so fastidious! " The old voice scaled up hysterically. "Nothing could ever make me believe she did it! Like a daughter to me, a daughter! She didn't do it! I will say it to my dying day! "

Mme. Storey smiled kindly.

"Your feelings do you credit, Mrs. Batten; still I hope you won't show them so plainly before the jury. "

"The—Jury! " whispered Mrs. Batten, scared and sobered.

"Because if you let them see how fond you are of Miss Dean they won't believe a word you say in her favor! "

"The jury! "

Mrs. Batten reiterated, staring before her as if she visualized the dreadful ordeal that awaited her.

"I will have to sit up there in the witness chair and take my oath before them all—and everybody looking at me—thousands—and lawyers asking me this and that a purpose to mix me up—"

She suddenly cried out:

"Oh I couldn't! I couldn't! I know I couldn't! I'm too nervous! I'd kill myself sooner than face that! "

The little woman's terror was so disproportionate to the thing she feared, that the strange thought went through my mind, perhaps it was she who killed Ashcomb Poor, or maybe she and the girl had done it together. I attended to what followed with a breathless interest. Meanwhile Mme. Storey was trying to quiet her.

"There now! There now, Mrs. Batten, don't distress yourself so. This is just an imaginary terror. It may never be necessary for you to go on the stand. Let's take a breathing spell to allow our nerves to quiet down. Have a cigarette? "

I stared at my employer, for at the moment this seemed like a very poor attempt at a joke. I ought to have known that Mme. Storey never did anything at such moments without a purpose. Mrs. Batten drew the remains of her dignity around her.

"Thank you, I don't indulge, " she said stiffly. She was pure mid-Victorian then.

Mme. Storey said teasingly:

"Come, now, Mrs. Batten! Not even in the privacy of your room? "

"Never! I'm not saying that I blame them that do if they like it; but in my day it wasn't considered nice. "

"Does Miss Dean smoke? " asked Mme. Storey with an idle air.

"I'm sure she does not! " answered Mrs. Batten earnestly. "I've been with her at all times and seasons, and I never saw her take one between her lips. There was no reason she should hide it from me. Besides, the maids never picked up any cigarette ends in her room. They're keen on such things. "'

"You have the reputation of being a very tidy person, haven't you, Mrs. Batten? " asked Mme. Storey. "They tell me you are a regular New England housekeeper. "

By this time I had guessed from Mme. Storey's elaborately careless air that this apparently meaningless questioning was tending to a well-defined point. The old lady glanced at her in a bewildered way, but she could see nothing behind this harmless remark.

"Why, yes, " she said,

"I suppose I do like to see things clean—real clean. And everything in its proper place. "

"Who does up your room? " went on Mme. Storey in the purring voice that always means danger—for somebody.

My heart began to beat.

"I do it myself, always, " answered the little woman unsuspectingly.

"I don't like the maids messing among my things. I like my room just so. I always sweep and dust and put things in order myself, and I mean to do so until I take to my bed for the last time. "

"Every day? " asked Mme. Storey, flicking the ash off her cigarette.

"Every day, most certainly. " Mme. Storey drawled in a voice as sweet as honey.

"Well, then, Mrs. Batten, who was it that was smoking cigarettes in your room the night that Ashcomb Poor was killed? "

The little old woman's jaw dropped, the rosy cheeks grayed, her eyes were like a sick woman's. Presently the hanging lip began to tremble piteously. I could not bear to look at her.

"I—I don't know what you're talking about, " she stuttered.

"You have not answered my question, " Mme. Storey said mildly.

"Nobody—nobody was smoking in my room. "

Mme. Storey turned to me.

"Miss Brickley, please get me the exhibits in the Poor case that I asked you to put away. "

Hastening into the next room I procured the things from the safe. When I returned neither of the two had changed position. From the envelope that I handed her, Mme. Storey shook the cigarette butts.

"These were found in your room early the next morning, " she said to Mrs. Batten. "In the little brass bowl on the window-sill. "

"All kinds of people were in the house that morning, " stammered the little woman with a desperate air, "police, detectives, goodness knows who! How do I know who passed through my room? "

"It was scarcely one who passed through, " said Mme. Storey. "He or she must have lingered some time—long enough, that is, to smoke seven cigarettes. See! "

She counted them before the old woman's fascinated eyes.

"I don't know how they came there. I don't know how they came there! " wailed the latter.

Mme. Storey spread the cigarette ends in a row.

"They are plain tip cigarettes, " she said, "so I assume they are a man's. Women prefer cork tips or straw tips, because lip rouge sticks and comes off on the paper. What gentleman visited you, Mrs. Batten? "

"There was nobody, nobody! " was the faint answer. "Why do you torment me? "

"There's no harm in having a visitor, surely. Your son, perhaps, a nephew, a brother—even a husband. Women do have them, Mrs. Batten. "

"Everybody knows I have no family. "

"A friend, then. Where's the harm? "

"There was nobody there. "

Mme. Storey examined the cigarette ends anew.

"One of them is long enough to show the name of the brand, " she said. "Army and Navy. One might guess that they were smoked by a man in the service. " The harried little woman gave her a glance of fresh terror. Delicately picking up one of the butts, Mme. Storey smelled of the unburned end.

"The tobacco is of a superior and expensive grade, " she remarked. "Evidently an officer's cigarette. But of what branch of the service? That is the question. "

She fixed the trembling little soul with her compelling gaze and asked abruptly:

"Was he an aviator, Mrs. Batten? "

A terrified cry escaped Mrs. Batten.

"I see he was, " said Mme. Storey.

Mrs. Batten was gazing at Mme. Storey as if the evil one himself confronted her. Answering that look of awed terror, my employer said quietly:

"No, there is no magic in it, Mrs. Batten. As a matter of fact, later that morning I found in the field across the brook at the foot of the garden marks in the earth showing where an airplane had alighted, and had later arisen again. I was only putting two and two together, you see. "

The little woman, seemingly incapable of speech, sat there with her hands clasped as if imploring for mercy. It was very affecting.

Mme. Storey went on:

"Upon consulting an expert in aviation I learned that such tracks could have been made by none other than one of the new Bentley-Critchard machines, of which there are as yet only half a dozen in service, and those all at Camp Tasker, which is only fifteen miles from Grimstead—a few minutes flight. All I lack is the name of the aviator who visited you. Who was he, Mrs. Batten? "

The little woman moistened her lips and whispered in a kind of dry cackle:

"I don't know. No one came. "

"You might as well tell me, " Mme. Storey said patiently. "It would not be difficult to find out at Camp Tasker, you know. There cannot be many officers accustomed to driving that new type. "

A groan broke from the little old woman. She covered her face with her hands.

"You are too much for me, " she murmured.

"It was Lieutenant George Grantland. "

I got out of my chair and sat down again, staring at the woman like a zany. Grantland! Eddie's hero! The popular idol of the day!

Mme. Storey was no less astonished than I.

"Quick, Bella! The morning paper! "

I hastened and got it for her. There was his name on the front page, of course, as it had been in every edition during the past two days.

Mme. Storey read out the head-lines:

GRANTLAND AT CHICAGO LAST NIGHT

Flew from Now Orleans Yesterday

Expected to land at Camp Tasker this A. M. Has circumnavigated the entire country east of the Mississippi in little more than three days. The bold young flier's endurance test a success in every particular.

Great ovations tendered him at every landing.

Meanwhile the wretched little old lady was weeping bitterly and wailing over and over:

"I promised not to tell! I promised not to tell! "

"Promised whom? " asked Mme. Storey.

"Philippa. "

"Well, you needn't distress yourself so, Mrs. Batten. If you love this girl, bringing the man's name into the case isn't going to hurt her chances any. "

Mrs. Batten had forgotten all caution now.

"But if you convict him, " she sobbed, "it will kill Philippa just the same. "

"Aha! " murmured Mme, Storey to herself; "so that's the way the wind lies. "

She looked at the old woman oddly.

"So Grantland did it? "

Mrs. Batten flung up her arms.

"I don't know! " she burst out, and at least that cry rang true. "I haven't eaten. I haven't slept since it happened. I'm nearly out of my mind with thinking about it! "

Mme. Storey whispered privately to me to call up Camp Tasker. If I could succeed in getting a message to Lieutenant Grantland I was to ask him to come to her office at once on a matter of the greatest importance concerning Miss Philippa Dean. Through the open door I could hear her asking Mrs. Batten to forgive her for tormenting her.

"But you know you came here determined not to tell me the truth, " she said.

In a few minutes I was able to report that I had got a message to Lieutenant Grantland, who had but just landed from his plane, and that he had promised to be in Mme. Storey's office within an hour.

Mrs. Batten was quiet again—quiet and wary. Poor little soul, now that one understood better, one couldn't help but admire her gallantry in lying to save her friends.

"Tell us about Lieutenant Grantland's visit, " Mme. Storey said encouragingly.

"There's nothing much to tell, " was the cautious answer. "He came to see Miss Philippa? "

"Yes. "

"He had been before? "

"Oh, yes; a number of times. "

"Did Miss Philippa know he was coming that night? "

"Yes. He had telephoned just before dinner. It was to say good-by before starting on the big flight. "

"What time did he come? "

"About nine. "

"Tell me about it in your own way. "

Mrs. Batten shook her head.

"You must question me, " she said warily. "I don't know what it is you want to know. "

Mme. Storey and I smiled, the old soul's equivocation was so transparent.

"Did Lieutenant Grantland always come in his plane? " my employer asked.

"No, that was the first time by plane. "

"Didn't the noise, of his engine attract attention at the house? "

"No; he shut it off and come down without a sound. "

"How could he see to land in the dark? "

"He came just before it got too dark to see. "

"But couldn't you see him land from the house? "

"No. He came down at the top of the field which is hidden from the house by the trees along the brook. "

"Then how could he get away in the dark? "

"He had the whole length of the field to rise from. "

"But in starting his engine didn't it make a great noise? "

"I don't know. We didn't notice it. "

"Did you go to meet him? "

"I, no. "

"Miss Philippa went? "

"Yes. "

"And brought him back to the house? "

"Yes. "

"Right away? "

Mrs. Batten bridled.

"I don't see what that—"

"Well what time did they get to the house? "

"About half past nine. "

"How did they get in? "

"I turned off the burglar-alarm and let them in the garden door. "

"What happened then? "

"Nothing! " said Mrs. Batten with an air which said:

"You're not going to get anything out of me! "

"Well, where did they go in the house? "

"They came into my room. They always sat there. "

"You left them there? "

"No, I stayed. Miss, Philippa always had me there when he came. So that nobody could have any excuse to talk. That shows you the kind of girl she was! "

"Very commendable. Go on. "

"There isn't anything to tell. There we sat as cozy and friendly as could be in my little room. I don't remember anything particular that was said. I wouldn't tell it if I did, for it was just their own matters. At ten o'clock I brought out a little supper I had made ready. The lieutenant was always hungry—like a boy. That's all. "

"What time did he leave? "

"At midnight. "

"That is, when Mrs. Poor got home? "

"Yes. "

"How did you get him out of the house?

"Mrs. Batten bridled again.

"There wasn't any getting out about it. He walked out of the same door that he came in. When I went to the front door to answer the bell I left the passage door open. When I switched on the light in the hall that was to tell them the burglar-alarm was off. Then Miss Philippa let the lieutenant out of the door from the back hall into the garden. "

"What was the necessity for all this secrecy, Mrs. Batten? Miss Philippa was treated like a member of the family. "

Mrs. Batten was very uncomfortable.

"Well, there was no necessity for it, so to speak, " she said. "But it seems natural for young lovers to wish to meet in secret, to avoid talk and all that. "

"And a moment after the lieutenant had gone you and Mrs. Poor discovered the murder? "

"Yes, but that isn't to say—"

"Of course it isn't! Up to that moment you yourself had no suspicion that there had been a tragedy in the house? "

"No, indeed! No, indeed! "

"After Miss Philippa let him out she presumably returned through the passage. That would explain how she came to be so close at hand when Mrs. Poor cried out. "

"I suppose so. But there's no harm in that. "

"Certainly not. But why was there so much lying, Mrs. Batten? Why did she tell me she had been in her room all evening? Why did you tell me you were alone in your room? "

"I couldn't give it away that she had been entertaining him. "

"Why not, if it was all regular and above board? "

"Well—well, I said I wouldn't tell. "

My employer became thoughtful.

Mrs. Batten, watching her, began to fidget again. Suddenly Mme. Storey said:

"Mrs. Batten, did Lieutenant Grantland know that Ashcomb Poor had been pestering Miss Philippa? "

"No! " answered Mrs. Batten breathlessly—but the terrified glance that accompanied it told its own tale.

"Now, Mrs. Batten, you're fibbing again! What's the use when your face is a mirror to your soul? "

The little body hung her head.

"Yes, he knew, " she murmured. "He had heard some gossip or something. He was furious when he came. Wanted to march right into the library and tax Mr. Poor with itto 'knock his block off, ' he said. We had a time quieting him down. The only thing that influenced him was when Miss Philippa said the scandal would injure her. "

"But you did quiet him down? "

"Yes. We were all as happy and pleasant as possible together. Then we had our supper. "

Mme. Storey fell silent for a while. Her grave and thoughtful glance seemed to inspire the little old woman with a fresh terror. Mrs. Batten struggled to her feet.

"I must go now, " she said tremulously.

"I've been away too long. They won't know what's become of me. "

"Sit down, Mrs. Batten, " said Mme. Storey quietly. The other's voice began to scale up again.

"I won't answer any more questions! " she cried. "Not another one! I can't! I'm in no fit state! I don't know what I'm saying! It's not fair to keep at me, and keep at me! "

"Sit down, Mrs. Batten, " repeated the grave voice.

The old woman dropped into a chair, weeping bitterly.

"Did Miss Philippa leave the room at any time during your party? "

This was evidently the very question Mrs. Batten dreaded.

"Oh, why do you plague me so? " she cried.

"You know the truth has got to come out. Better tell me than a roomful of men. " Mrs.

Batten gave up.

"Yes, she did, " she wailed.

"How long was she gone? "

"I don't know. Just a little while. Not more than ten minutes. "

"And did Lieutenant Grantland leave the room at any time? "

"Yes. "

"How long was he gone? "

"He left right after her, and got back just before her. "

"Ah! What was the occasion of their leaving the room? "

"The bell rang in the pantry. I went to see what it was. The indicator showed a call from the library, It wasn't my place to answer the bell, but I did so because I was afraid if I didn't Mr. Poor might come back. He was at his writing-table. I thought he had been drinking a little. "

"Why did you think so? "

"His face was flushed. He had a fumy look. He said, 'Will you please ask Miss Dean if she will be good enough to help me out for a little while. I have two or three important letters to get off, and I have such a cramp in my hand I can't write them myself. '"

"Did you believe this, Mrs. Batten? "

"N—no, madame. Not with that look—an ugly look to a woman. "

"What did you do? "

"Well of course I couldn't say anything to him. I just went away as if I was going to do what he wanted. I went back to my room. I was hoping maybe he'd forget. But they saw from my face that something had happened—"

"That open countenance! " murmured Mme. Storey.

"And they gave me no rest until I told them what he wanted. The lieutenant flared up again and said she should not go. Said he'd go instead and write his letters on his face. But she persuaded him not to. She knew how to manage him. She said she must go in order to avoid trouble. She said nothing could happen to her as long as the lieutenant was there in the house to protect her. So she went. "

"Alone? "

"Yes. But when she was gone, he could not rest. In spite of all I could do to stop him, he went after her. I stayed there sitting in my room—helpless. Every minute I expected to hear a terrible quarrel but all was quiet. I could scarcely stand it. I would have gone, too, to see; but my old legs were trembling so they would not carry me. "

"You heard no sound while they were gone? "

"None whatever, madame. "

"But there were three heavy doors between you and the library. "

"The library door stood open all evening. "

"But it may have been closed then. "

Mrs. Batten wrung her hands.

"It can't be! It cant be, " she cried. "That young pair—so proud, so beautiful, so loving. "

"Well, murder is not always so detestable a crime, " observed Madame. Storey enigmatically. "Did they come back together? "

The old woman shook her head.

"He came back first. "

"How did he look? "

"Nothing out of the way. No different from when be left. "

"You mean, his face was set and hard? "

"Yes, but he always looked like that when Mr. Poor's name was mentioned. "

"What did he say? "

"He said, 'Where's Philippa? ' I just shook my head. He turned around to go look for her, but met her coming in the door. They spoke to each other. "

"What did they say? "

"It was in whispers. I could not hear. "

Mme. Storey fixed the little woman hard with her gaze.

"Mrs. Batten! " she said warningly.

But this time the housekeeper was able to meet it. She spread out her hands in a gesture that was not without dignity.

"I have told you everything, madame. You know as much as I do now. "

"And nothing happened after that? "

"No, madame. We sat down to supper. Mr. Poor's name was not mentioned again. "

"Either one of them could have done it, " remarked Mme. Storey thoughtfully.

Mrs. Batten wiped away her fast-falling tears.

CHAPTER 7.

Lieutenant Grantland was prompt to his engagement.

Why is it that aviators, or nearly all aviators, are such superb young men? I suppose the answer is obvious enough; it is the young men with the shining eyes and the springy bodies that are naturally attracted to the air. However that may be, the mere sight of an aviator is enough to take a girl's breath away.

As for George Grantland, he was simply the handsomest young man I ever saw. When he came in how I longed to be comely just for one second, in order to win an interested glance from him. Alas! His eyes merely skated over me. In his close-fitting uniform and marvelously turned leggings he was as graceful as Mercury. At present, whether from fatigue or anxiety—or both his cheeks were drawn and gray. But his blue eyes were resolute, and he kept his chin up.

You can imagine Eddie's feelings. He had brought the lieutenant upstairs all agog, and now stood just within the door, staring at his idol, and fairly panting with excitement. I was obliged to push the boy out into the hall by main strength and shut the door after him.

I took Lieutenant Grantland directly into Mme. Storey's room. Her glance brightened at the sight of him just as any woman's would. She had mercy on me and nodded to me to remain in the room. Mrs. Batten, I should state, was still with us. Mme. Storey had put her in the back room to rest and compose herself.

"Thank you for coming so promptly, " Mme. Storey said, extending her hand.

The young man blushed painfully.

"I cannot shake hands, " he said bluntly.

Mme. Storey's eyebrows went up.

"Why? " she asked, smiling.

"You will not want to shake hands when you know. "

Mme. Storey shrugged and smiled at him with an expression I could not fathom—a quizzical expression.

"Well, sit down, " she said.

He would not unbend.

"Thank you, I cannot stay. "

"Well, anyway, allow me to congratulate you on your flight. "

He bowed. Mme. Storey went on:

"My secretary tells me she got a message to you just as you were landing. I assume that you heard nothing during your flight of what was happening here. "

"Not a word! " he said.

"But Camp Tasker was buzzing with it. I heard everything there. "

"Then we need not go into lengthy explanations, " said Mme. Storey. "I need only say that Assistant District Attorney Barron has done me the honor to consult me in regard to this matter. That is where I come in. As for my secretary, she is acquainted with the details of the case, you need have no hesitancy in speaking before her. I would like to ask you a few, questions, if you please. "

"There is no need, " he said, standing very stiffly.

"It was I who killed Ashcomb Poor. "

My heart went down sickeningly—not that I blamed him at all; but at the thought of that splendid young fellow being subjected to the rigor of the law; his career spoiled; that proud head brought low in a prison cell! I don't know what Mme. Storey felt upon hearing his avowal. Her glance betrayed nothing.

"I never dreamed that they would dare arrest her, " the young man went on with a break in his voice, "or I never should have gone away. I can never forgive myself that. "

"Well, sit down, " said Mme. Storey for the second time.

He shook his head.

"I am on my way to police headquarters to give myself up. "

"Oh, but not so fast! " objected my employer. "There are many things to be considered. Meet Mr. Barron here. You will be at a better advantage. "

"I have no desire to make terms, " he said indifferently.

"Then let me make them for you. Or lay it to a woman's vanity, if you like. I found you first. Let me hand you over to the district attorney's office. "

"Just as you like, " he said. Turning to me Mme.

Storey said:

"Please call up the district attorney's office and tell Mr. Barron that important new evidence has turned up in the Ashcomb Poor case. Ask him if he will bring Miss Dean up here. "

At the words "bring Miss Dean" a spasm of pain passed over the young man's face.

"Do you think he will? " I murmured, thinking of Mr. Barron's former objections.

"What he did once he can do again, " Mme. Storey said lightly. "Curiosity is a strong, impelling force. "

She added in a lower tone:

"Mrs. Poor is at the Madagascar Hotel. Ask her to come, too. Then we'll have all the material witnesses. "

Then to the aviator:

"If you came here the moment you landed you haven't had anything to eat. "

"I don't require anything, thanks, " he muttered.

"Nonsense! You have a severe ordeal before you. You must prepare for it in any way that you can. "

To make a long story short I ordered in a meal. It arrived after I had finished my telephoning, and both Mme. Storey and I saw to it that the young man did justice to the repast. Not withstanding his situation he developed an excellent appetite.

It struck me at the time that we were treating him more like the returned prodigal than a self-confessed murderer; but good looks such as his are like a magic talisman in the possessor's favor. What would any woman have cared what he had done? How delightful it was to see a better color return to his cheeks. And how grateful he was for cigarettes!

Mr. Barron brought two plainclothes men and Miss Dean in his own automobile. We received, them in the outer office, and Mme. Storey insisted on allowing the girl to enter her room alone. When the door was opened and Philippa saw who was waiting within, a dreadful low cry broke from her that wrung our very hearts.

Mme. Storey closed the door behind her, and no one ever knew what took place between those two unhappy young persons. While we waited Mr. Barron besieged Mme. Storey with questions which she smilingly refused to answer, merely saying:

"Wait and see! "

They were not together long. Lieutenant Grantland opened the door. His face was stony. In a chair behind him the girl was weeping bitterly. It looked as if they had quarreled.

He said to Mme. Storey:

"We must not keep you out of your own room. "

Mme. Storey, Mr. Barron and I went in. My employer, much against Mr. Barron's wishes, insisted that the plain-clothes men be required to wait in the outer office.

"I fancy there are enough of us here to frustrate any attempt at an escape, " she said dryly.

Mrs. Batten was called in. She was in a great taking at the sight of Philippa and the young officer, but the former kissed her tenderly, and the young man shook hands with her. When we all seated ourselves the place instantly took on the aspect of a courtroom.

I am sure I am quite safe in saying that every one of us—except possibly my inscrutable employer—was shaking with excitement. Our faces were pale and streaked with anxiety. Mme. Storey sat at her table and I was in my usual place at her left.

Mr. Barron sat at her right, while Miss Dean, Lieutenant Grantland and Mrs. Batten faced us in that order. Before anything was said there was a knock at the door, and upon being bidden to open it Eddie ushered in a heavily shrouded figure that all knew for Mrs. Poor, though her face was invisible.

I expect Eddie would have given some years of his youthful life to be allowed to remain, but a glance from Mme. Storey sent him flying.

Mr. Barron hastened to place a chair for Mrs. Poor next to Mrs. Batten. The young soldier arose and bowed stiffly.

Philippa turned her head away from the newcomer with a painful blush. Mme. Storey said in a voice devoid of all emotion:

"Lieutenant Grantland wishes to make a statement. "

Grantland was still on his feet.

He came to attention and said in a low, steady voice:

"I wish to say that it was I who shot Ashcomb Poor. "

The widow started violently.

One could imagine the piercing gaze she must have bent on the speaker through her veil.

Philippa Dean covered her face with her hands, and Mrs. Batten began to weep audibly.

Mr. Barron's face was a study in astonishment and discomfiture, Mme. Storey's a mask. Mme. Storey said:

"Please tell us the circumstances. "

"Wait a minute, " stammered the assistant district attorney. "It is my duty to inform you that anything you say may be used against you. "

"I quite understand that, " said Grantland.

"I must have a record of his statement! " went on Mr. Barron excitedly.

"Miss Brickley will take notes of everything that transpires, " said Mme. Storey. "Please proceed, lieutenant. "

He spoke in a level, quiet voice, with eyes straight ahead, looking at none of us.

"I was calling on Miss Dean to whom I am—to whom I was engaged to be married. We were with Mrs. Batten—in her sitting-room. Mr. Poor sent to Miss Dean to ask if she would write some letters for him. I had heard certain things—things that led me to suspect that this was merely a pretext. Anyway it was no part of her duties to look after his correspondence. I didn't want her to go. But she persuaded me that it would be better for her to go. And she went. But when she left the room I became very uneasy. I followed her. Down a passage, and across the main hall of the house. The hall was dark.

"The man was in a room off the hall—a library, I suppose you'd call it. The door stood open, and from the hall I could see all that took place. Mr. Poor, with many apologies, was repeating his request that

Miss Dean write some letters for him. He made believe his hand was cramped. But he looked at her in a way—in a way that made my blood hot. I think he had been drinking. I could see that Miss Dean was frightened. I was at the point of interfering then, but I heard her ask him to excuse her while she got a handkerchief, and she came out and ran upstairs. She did not see me in the hall.

"Well, I remained there watching him. The expression on his face as he sat there waiting for her to return drove me wild. "

"But he was sitting with his back to the hall, " interrupted Mme. Storey. "How could you see his face? "

"There was a mirror over the fireplace hung at such an angle that his face was reflected in it. "

"But if you could see him in it could be not see you? "

"No, I was standing too far back in the dark hall. "

"Go on. "

"The look on his face conveyed an insult no man could bear. I went in and shot him, that's all. "

Philippa Dean struggled to her feet. From her lips broke a cry none of us will ever forget.

"It's not true! It was I who did it! He knows it was I. He's trying to shield me! "

She could go no further, but stood, struggling to control the dry sobbing that tore her breast. None of the rest of us stirred. Grantland did not look at her. One could see that he dared not.

"She knows it was I, " he said stonily.

With a great effort Philippa regained a measure of control.

"Listen! Listen! " she cried desperately. I will tell the truth now. "Mr. Poor sent for me. He asked me to take some letters. He looked at me in such a way I was afraid—afraid. I asked him to excuse me while I got a handkerchief. I went upstairs. But it was my pistol that I went for. I was so afraid they would meet and fight. I got my pistol. I came down stairs again. I shot him. Lieutenant Grantland wasn't there at all! "

"I was there! " cried Grantland. "Ask Mrs. Batten. Mrs. Batten, didn't I follow her? "

"Oh! Oh! Oh! " wailed the little body.

"Yes, you followed her. "

"And if I was not there how could I have know about the handkerchief? " he demanded.

By this time Philippa had nerved herself. She faced him out fearlessly. Never have I seen anything like that, look, so hard, so full of pain.

"Well, if you were there you didn't wait till I got back. You weren't there when I got back, were you? Answer that. "

"No, " he admitted, "but—"

She wouldn't let him go on.

"Why should I have wanted a handkerchief at such a moment? It was my pistol I went for, and I got it, and I came downstairs and shot him. "

"Without warning? " Grantland demanded in his turn.

"No. I sat down and made ready to take his letters. But he had no letters to dictate, of course. He put his hand on my shoulder and I—I shot him. "

How could you shoot him in the back when you were sitting beside him? "

"I reached around behind him and shot him. "

"Where did you have the pistol? "

"Hidden in the bosom of my waist. "

"The waist you wore that night was closed in front. "

"Pooh! What do you know about such things? You never notice what I have on. Mrs. Batten, wasn't the waist I wore that night buttoned in front? "

The little body was completely distracted.

"Yes—no—I don't know I can't remember! " she wailed.

"Now answer me, " cried Philippa to Grantland.

"How could you get into the room when the man was sitting there watching in the mirror for my return? "

"I dropped to my knees out of range of his vision and crept in. "

The girl's eyes flashed at him.

"Do you mean to tell all these people that you, an officer in the uniform of the United States, crawled in on hands and knees like a thug and shot the man in the back? "

Grantland's head dropped on his breast; a dark flush overspread his face, he gritted his teeth until the muscles stood out in lumps on either side his jaw.

"It is the truth, " he muttered. "I looked on him as a kind of wild beast against whom any measures were justifiable. "

The girl passionately appealed to the rest of us.

"Look at him! Look at him! " she cried. "Anyone could see he is lying! "

The spectacle of the two lovers cross-examining each other; facing each other down with hard, inimical glances; each desperately striving to pull down the other's tale, was the strangest and most dreadful scene I ever expect to witness. The young man stubbornly raised his head, and his glance bore hers down. He had better command of himself than she.

"Your story could not be true, " he said firmly. "You were not more than half a minute behind me in returning to Mrs. Batten's room. "

"Half a minute was long enough to pull the trigger, " she retorted.

A new thought struck Grantland.

"You could not have returned that way at all, " he said. "You must have come down the back stairs. I remember now that as you came into the room you appeared from the rear of the house. "

"Too bad you didn't think of that before, " she rejoined scornfully.

"Your tardy recollection will not deceive Mme. Storey or this gentleman. This is all wasting time anyway. You have not explained the most important thing of all. "

"What's that? " he asked sullenly.

"How did you get hold of my pistol? "

She thought she had him there, but he instantly retorted:

"You gave it to me yourself a week before to have it fixed. I had had it fixed, and I was bringing it back to you that night. "

"Now I have caught you! " cried the girl with wildly shining eyes. "You had returned my pistol to me two days before that night, and Mrs. Batten was present when you handed it to me! "

She whirled around.

"Mrs. Batten didn't you see him return my pistol to me two days before that night? "

The little woman, unable to speak, nodded her head.

"Now, who's lying? " cried Philippa.

The young aviator never flinched.

"That wasn't your pistol I gave you two days before, " he said coolly. "That was a pistol I borrowed from the dealer while yours was being repaired. I got it for you because I believed after what I'd heard that you ought not to be without the means to defend yourself. "

"Why didn't you tell me all this at the time? " she demanded.

"Because I would have had to explain why I got you the pistol, and I didn't want to alarm you unnecessarily. "

"Fine tale! " she said with curling lip but her assurance was failing her.

"How about the two little marks on the barrel that identified the pistol as mine? "

"That is the dealer's private mark to protect himself. It appears on all the weapons that he handles. "

"Well, if it was really my pistol that you say you shot the man with why did you leave it there to incriminate me? "

"I thought you had only to produce the one you had in order to clear yourself. "

"It's not true! No other was found! "

"There was no other. What did you want to leave the pistol there for anyway to make trouble. "

"I thought it would be regarded as a suicide. " Philippa had regained her assurance.

"Do you expect these people to believe that with your knowledge of weapons you thought you could shoot the man through the back and have anybody think he did it himself? "

Grantland showed some confusion.

"Well, I was excited, " he said sullenly.

"One can't think of everything. " The girl smiled scornfully. "I've no more to say, " she said abruptly. "These people will not need any help in deciding who is telling the truth. "

She sat down. What the others thought of this confession and counter-confession I cannot say.

I believed Philippa was telling the truth. My employer's face was like a tinted, ivory mask.

"Have you anything more to say? " she asked Grantland. He shook his head.

"Mr. Barron, do you wish to put any questions? "

"I think not, " he answered, with a casual air that did not conceal his triumph. "I see no reason to alter my original opinion. Lieutenant Grantland's motives do him credit, but his story simply does not hold water. Leaving aside all other considerations it is preposterous to suppose that after shooting the man in the way he describes he could fly away and leave the two women to their fate. "

Philippa looked gratefully toward him.

What a strange, topsy-turvey situation that she should actually thank him for expressing his belief in her guilt! My employer said in the silky tones that always portended danger:

"I must differ with you, Mr. Barron. Lieutenant Grantland has explained how he thought he had insured Miss Dean's safety. On the other hand it is incredible to suppose that a gently reared girl, after having killed a man, could sit down and sup with her two friends as if nothing had happened. A man might, a soldier, but this girl, never! And afterward allow him, her only protector to leave her without a word! "

"I had to let him go, " sobbed Philippa. "His reputation was staked on that flight! "

I noticed at this point that Mrs. Poor's foot was nervously tapping the floor.

In my concern for the two young people, it had not occurred to me what a harrowing business all this must have been for the widow.

"No, " said Mme. Storey to Mr. Barron, "you have done me the honor to consult me in this case. I must ask you to put Lieutenant Grantland under arrest. I pledge myself to justify it directly. "

Grantland fairly beamed on my employer. I wondered mightily what she was up to. Poor Philippa seemed on the verge of a collapse.

"But how—why—on what grounds? " demanded the puzzled prosecutor.

Mme. Storey's next words fell like icy drops:

"At the proper moment I will produce an eye-witness to the affair who will swear that Lieutenant Grantland shot Ashcomb Poor. "

"You lie! "

This scream—for scream it was—from a new direction, almost completed the demoralization of our nerves. Every eye turned toward Mrs. Poor.

She had leaped to her feet and had thrown her veil back, The pale, proud face was working with intense emotion, her hands were dragging at her bodice, she had lost every vestige of control—a dreadful sight.

"It's a conspiracy! " she cried shrilly. "To railroad him—with his consent! They staged it here together. Can't you all see? That's why we were brought here! "

Mme. Storey turned to the hysterical woman with seeming surprise.

"Why, Mrs. Poor, what do you know about it? "

Under that cold glance the woman suddenly collapsed in her chair. Her eyes sickened with terror. The strident voice declined to a whisper.

"Of course—of course I don't know, " she stuttered. "I am simply overwrought. All this—all this has been too much for me. I am simply overwrought. I beg your pardon. I will retire—if some one will help me to my car. "

Mr. Barron made a move to go to her, but Mme. Storey laid hand on his arm and looked at him significantly. He fell back in his chair muttering, "My God! "

At Mme. Storey's mention of a new witness Philippa had sagged down in her chair. Little Mrs. Batten had flown to her, and now knelt beside her with an arm around the girl.

Grantland was staring at Mrs. Poor with a strange, perplexed frown.

"Don't go, Mrs. Poor, " said Mme. Storey softly. "Help us to throw a little light on this baffling matter. "

Mrs. Poor made an attempt to draw her accustomed garments of pride and aloofness about her, but they would no longer serve. She shivered under our glances like a naked woman. Mme. Storey proceeded:

"How long have you known Lieutenant Grantland? "

"About two years, " was the reply.

"Ah, that is longer than Miss Dean has known him, isn't it? "

"Yes. "

"Miss Dean met Lieutenant Grantland in your house? "

"Yes. "

"Formerly you took a great interest in Lieutenant Grantland? "

"I liked him, if that is what you mean. We were friends. "

"Great friends? "

"That is such a vague phrase. I advised him as I could out of my greater experience. "

"Like an elder sister? "

"If you like. "

"Did you notice any change in him after he met Miss Dean? "

"No. "

"But he stopped coming to see you. "

"Well, yes. I saw him less often. "

"But he was still coming to the house? "

"So it seems. "

"Did you know they were engaged? "

"Yes. "

"How? "

"Gossip, rumor. "

"He did not tell you? "

"No. "

Mme. Storey turned unexpectedly to Mrs. Batten.

"Mrs. Batten, " she said, "why did Lieutenant Grantland come to see Miss Dean secretly? Quick, the truth! "

The little body could not resist that sharp command.

She glanced in a scared way at her mistress, and the truth came tumbling out involuntarily.

"She—she had taken a fancy to him. They did not wish to anger her. "

"That is sufficient, " said Mme. Storey.

Mrs. Poor struggled to her feet.

"Servants' gossip! " she cried. "This is outrageous! I will not stay to be insulted! "

Mme. Storey rose too, and said in a tone oddly compounded of scorn and pity:

"What's the use, Mrs. Poor? You have passed the limit of a woman's endurance. Tell the assistant district attorney who killed your husband. "

The other woman with a last effort threw her head back, and tried to face Mme. Storey down—meanwhile her ashy cheeks and trembling lips told their own tale.

"How should I know? " she cried. "How dare you take such a tone to me? Do you presume to accuse me? Oh, this is too funny! "

Her laugh had a shocking ring.

"You know very well I was performing at the club when it happened. Hundreds saw me there. I returned home with my servants. Ask them! "

"I know all this, " said Mme. Storey with a bored air, "but that's only the beginning of the story. Sit down and I'll tell the rest. "

Mrs. Poor obeyed—simply because her legs would not support her.

As Mme. Storey proceeded the other woman let her veil fall over her face. Her hands convulsively gripped the arms of her chair.

Mme. Storey sat down and drew from the drawer of her table the several bits of evidence in connection with the case. She had in addition a program of the pageant given at the Pudding Stone Club. Consulting this she said:

"You made your first appearance in the second tableau as Starving Russia, " she said. "This was at nine fifteen. Upon leaving the stage your maid dressed you for your second appearance. This consumed about twenty-five minutes. You then went out into the audience to view the performance. Your maid joined the other servants in the part of the grounds reserved for them. You had told her you would not need her again.

"While everybody was looking at a tableau you slipped into the shrubbery surrounding the open air theater and made your way to your car. You are an expert chauffeur, as everybody knows. You drove it home. You did not turn in at the main gate but at the lower entrance leading to the service door. You did not drive up to the house, but left the car just inside the gate and walked to the house. The tracks made by the car were found where you had run it just inside the gate, and later backed it out into the road again. It was identified as your car by certain peculiarities in the tires.

"You went to one of the French windows of the library—to be exact, it was the second window from the front door. In order to reach the sill you had to make one step in the soft mold of the flower bed. You turned around on the sill, and stooping over, with your hand you brushed loose earth over the print of your foot. But a slight depression was left there, and by carefully brushing the loose dirt away again I was able to lay bare the deep print made by your slipper.

"I assume that you tapped on the window, and that your husband, seeing you, turned off the burglar alarm and let you in. This would be about ten o'clock, or just as the other three persons in the house were sitting down to supper in Mrs. Batten's room. Perhaps you glanced through the window of that room as you passed by on the drive. What you said to your husband, of course, I do not know. My guess is that you accounted for your unexpected return by saying that an unforeseen request for a contribution had been made on you. At any rate he sat down at his writing-table and drew out his checkbook. As he dated the stub you shot him in the back with Miss Dean's pistol which you had previously stolen from her bureau. "

A convulsive shudder passed through the frame of the woman in black. Mme. Storey continued in her sure, quiet voice:

"You had wrapped your right arm and the hand holding the pistol in many folds of a chiffon scarf. This was for the double purpose of concealing the weapon and of muffling the report. After the deed you tore off these wrappings, and, crumpling the scarf into a ball, threw it on the fire, which the servants have testified was burning in the room. But it must have opened up as it burned. At any rate a small piece fell outside the embers, and was not consumed. Here it is. The characteristic odor of gunpowder still clings to it faintly.

"My principal difficulty was to establish how you got out of the house. I suspected that you must have contrived some means of setting the burglar alarm behind you. The string box on Mr. Poor's desk furnished me with my clue. It was empty. When the last piece of string comes out of such a box, a man's instinctive act is to put a fresh ball in at once—if he has one. There were several spare balls in Mr. Poor's desk. Yet the box was empty. I may say that I subsequently found the length of string that you pulled out of that box in a tangled skein beside the road, where you threw it on your way back to the club. Here it is.

"When I examined the burglar alarm all was clear. A tiny staple had been driven into the floor under the switch. It was still there at nine o'clock of the morning after the murder when you had had no opportunity to remove it. You tied the string in a slip knot to the handle of the switch, passed the other end through the staple in the floor—this gave you the necessary downward pull on the handle. You then ran the string across the floor and passed it through the keyhole of the front door. This door locks with a spring lock, and the original keyhole is not used.

"You went out closing the door behind you. Your first light pull on the string set the alarm—the handle of the switch moved easily. A second and harder pull slipped the knot, and you drew the string through the keyhole. You returned to the club, arriving there in ample time for your second appearance as Victory at 10:50. "

An absolute silence filled the room. We glanced at one another in a dazed way, wondering if we dared credit what our ears had heard. Then suddenly joy flamed up in the faces of the two young people—the loveliest thing I have ever seen. But I turned away my head. We all did. We heard them cry each other's names.

"Philippa! "

"George! "

Presently Mme. Storey said:

"Mrs. Poor, are the facts not as I have stated? "

The wretched woman sat huddled in her chair like a demented person. I was glad her face was hidden. Suddenly she straightened up and cried out:

"Yes, it's true! It's true! I killed him! I shot him just as you say! Thank God! I've told it! I can sleep now! " Once the bonds of speech were broken, she could not stop herself.

"Yes, I killed him! I killed him! " she repeated over and over. "I couldn't stand it any longer! I'm not sorry for it! Who's going to blame me? What kind of a life did I lead? What kind of a wife was I? An object of scorn to my own servants! No one will ever know what I put up with. Oh, I know what they said, 'The proud, cold Mrs. Poor, she doesn't feel anything! ' Proud! Cold! Oh my God! When I was burning up! When I died a thousand deaths daily! What do gabbling women know of what such a woman as I can suffer! "

This was unspeakably painful for us to listen to. Mme. Storey looked significantly at Mr. Barron.

He, whose attitude toward Mrs. Poor had undergone a great change during the past few minutes, now stepped forward and touched her arm. She drew away from him with a sharp, new cry of terror.

"No! No! Not that! Not that! "

Throwing aside her veil again she turned to Grantland with outstretched arms.

"George, don't let them take me away! " she cried. "George, help me! Help me! "

The young man walked to the window.

Mrs. Poor was led out, still crying pitifully his name. Mme. Storey turned quickly to Mrs. Batten.

"Will you go with her? She needs a woman near. "

The good little body hurried after.

Grantland went back to Philippa. Drawing her hand under his arm he brought her up to Mme. Storey's table. After their terrible ordeal they were gravely happy, it seemed not to be necessary for these two to speak to each other; the look in their eyes told all. The young man said to my employer:

"How can we ever thank you? "

Mme. Storey put on a brusk air to hide the fact that she was moved.

"Nonsense! You owe me nothing! I got my reward in taking the wind out of the assistant district attorney's sails! "

"What a wonderful woman you are! " murmured the girl.

"That's what people always say" said Mme. Storey ruefully. "It makes me feel like a side-show. "

Philippa looked at her lieutenant.

"What a fool I was to believe he could have done it! "

He looked back.

"I was the bigger fool. "

"Wonderful liars, both of you! " said Mme. Storey dryly. "You had me guessing more than once. Like all really good liars, you stuck close to the, truth. His story was true up to the point where he said he crawled into the library on hands and knees. That was just a little overdone, lieutenant. As a matter of fact when Philippa didn't come back, you returned to the housekeeper's room to look for her. By the way, that touch about the second revolver was masterly. "

Grantland blushed.

Mme. Storey turned to Philippa.

"You told the truth up to the point where you said you got your pistol out of the drawer. It wasn't there, of course. After searching frantically for it, you were afraid to return to the library without it, and you stole down the back stairs, knowing you would be safe with your young man anyhow. "

They bade her a grateful farewell and went out. They made an uncommonly handsome pair. Mr. Barron returned to the room. He had a highly self-conscious air that betrayed him.

"Oh, I thought you'd gone, " said Mme. Storey.

"No, I sent Mrs. Poor downtown in her own car with my men. I'll follow directly. I wanted to speak to you. "

"Go ahead, " said Mme. Storey.

"It's a private matter, " he said with a venomous glance in my direction.

Mme. Storey, with a whimsical twinkle in her eye, signified that I might leave.

I knew she was going to turn on the dictograph. She had no mercy on that man. I heard him say:

"Well, Rose, I take off my hat to you! In this case you certainly beat me to it! I confess it. I couldn't say fairer than that. "

"It's not necessary to say anything, Walter. "

"But I want you to know the kind of fellow I am. I'm a generousminded man, Rosie. The trouble is you provoke me so I fly in a rage when I'm with you and you don't get the right idea of me. I'm gentle as a lamb if you take me right. "

"Well, I'm glad to hear that, Walter. "

"Take me for good, Rosie! You and I need each other. Your intuition is all right. With your intuition and my logic we'll make an unbeatable pair. I'll tell you all my cases, Rosie, and let you advise me. Honest, I will. Give me a smile, Rosie. I don't mean that kind of a smile. From the heart! You cut the ground from under my feet with that wicked little smile. Smile kindly on me, Rosie—"

It was indecent to listen to a man making such a fool of himself. I took the headpiece off and laid it down.

The next moment, Mr. Barron, very red about the gills, banged out of Mme. Storey's room, stamped across my office and downstairs. Mme. Storey rang for me. She was imperturbably lighting a cigarette.

"I'm ready to take up the Cornwall case, " she said.

"Bring me the papers from the file. "

THE END

Lightning Source UK Ltd.
Milton Keynes UK
UKHW010634230622
404860UK00001B/53

9 781006 972607